AIDEN

Aiden

THE KEATYN CHRONICLES: BOOK 9

JILLIAN DODD

Jillian Dodd Inc.
N. Redington Beach, FL

ISBN: 978-1-946793-00-3

Books by Jillian Dodd

The *USA TODAY* bestselling series,
The Keatyn Chronicles®
Stalk Me

Kiss Me

Date Me

Love Me

Adore Me

Hate Me

Get Me

Keatyn Unscripted

Hollywood Love Series
(A Keatyn Chronicles Spin off)
Fame

Power

Money

Sex

Love

That Boy Series
That Boy

That Wedding

That Baby

The Love Series
Vegas Love

Broken Love

Spy Girl Series
The Prince

The Eagle

The Society

I want to start Aiden's point of view off with the scene from *Get Me* where Keatyn finally tells Aiden the truth about who she is and why she lied. I think most readers were pretty shocked when he told Keatyn that he already knew.

He's quiet on the elevator, on the walk down the hall, and as we go into our room.

After the dirt, the No more lying, *and all the* You can tell me anythings, *I understand why.*

He has every right to be mad. I should've listened to my heart and told him. I had so many opportunities, going all the way back to that day in the chapel.

"Before you say anything, I need to tell you something," I blurt out.

He takes my hand and leads me over to the chaise, where we both sit down.

He lets go of my hand but I quickly grab it again, clinging to it like a life raft.

"I'm sorry I lied to you. There's a lot more to the story. I under-stand if you hate me. I deserve it. But you have to know that there were so many times I wanted to tell you. Remember the slutty video?

When Dawson and I broke up? I was taking him to meet my parents that weekend. I was going to tell him the truth. That's why I was so upset. I was more upset at myself for trusting the wrong person again than I was about us not dating. And that's why, after what happened with Chelsea, I forgave you but wouldn't see you. I couldn't lie to you anymore. I was in deep with you, and I knew that eventually I'd have to tell you, and that you'd hate me for lying. But then you brought me dirt and told me our pasts didn't matter."

Tears stream down my face, feeling cold against my flushed cheeks. "You have no idea how deeply that touched me. And it's why I let you come to St. Croix. I wasn't planning to go back to school. I didn't get closure with B. Everything with him—especially how I had to leave—has been so up the air and I didn't want to do that to you. I was going to give you closure, then send you back to school. And that's why I've been so tired all the time. At night, I'm either learning how to defend myself, or I'm flying back to California to mess with him, or I'm having online business meetings in an attempt to take over his company. It's not my friend who was being stalked and almost got kidnapped. It was me." I stop and mutter, "Shit."

Then I stand up and grab my clutch off the bed.

"What are you doing?" Aiden asks.

I pull out a piece of paper and hold it up in front of him. "This is the script I've been working on. In it, instead of truth-vomiting, I eloquently explain everything to you. I couldn't have sex with you until you knew."

I drop the piece of paper on the chaise, wondering why I'm even bothering.

He's not going to forgive me.

I might as well just grab my bags and go.

But he starts reading my script aloud.

"THE SETTING: HOTEL SUITE AFTER WINTER FORMAL.

AIDEN

(Opening a bottle of champagne)

KEATYN

(Lighting all the votive candles he thoughtfully
brought)
(They kiss)
(But then she looks nervous)
I need to tell you something.

AIDEN

(Sits on the edge of the bed)
What?

KEATYN

(Stands in front of him)
I've been lying to you. Actually, I've been lying
to everyone about something. And I need you to
know.

AIDEN

(Looks concerned)
Okay.

KEATYN

I came to Eastbrooke because I was being stalked.
My last name isn't Monroe. I'm Keatyn Douglas.
And my mom doesn't work in oil and gas. But she
is in France. And her name is Abby Johnston.

AIDEN

(Stands up in shock)"

Aiden stares at the script for a few moments then slowly sets it down. I can tell he's thinking; probably trying to figure out the nicest way to tell me to fuck off.

Instead, he stands up, takes two big steps toward me, and brushes a tear off my cheek. *"Life hasn't been following your scripts. You told me that once."*

"No, it hasn't."

"If it had worked out the way you planned—if you'd followed your script—right now is the point where life would have deviated from it."

"You wouldn't have stood up in shock?"

"No," he says, caressing my face. *"I would have said,* Baby, I already knew.*"*

"You what?! What do you mean?!"

"I mean I've known for quite a while who you really are."

"How?!"

"That day at the chapel, when you told me about your friend. I don't know. I just felt like you were talking about yourself. So I started googling stuff. The name Keatyn, California, stalker, famous parents. Somehow, eventually, I put in the right mix of words. About ten pages into an image search, I came across a photo of you and your mom. It was from a kids' awards show when you were probably twelve or thirteen."

"You've known this whole time and you let me lie to you?"

"Yeah, Boots, I did."

"Why?"

"Because I wanted to be the kind of guy you could trust. It's why I backed off. Why I told Riley about Dawson. I didn't want to see you hurt anymore. It's why I've told you so many times that you can tell me anything. That you could trust me. What I didn't realize before was that I needed to earn that trust. We had to build a strong foundation. I'm really glad you were planning to tell me tonight."

A lot of readers wondered when Aiden figured out the truth and why he didn't confront her about it. I think looking back, it's easy to tell where he figured it out. If you recall, he'd been pursuing Keatyn since she got to Eastbrooke, but suddenly he stopped and told her that he wanted them to be friends. I think a lot of readers thought this was sort of a ploy on his part. A way to spend time with her (and torture her with his godly smile) while she was dating Dawson. Or that he had given up. Or that he simply backed off because she was dating Dawson.

So, I'm going to let Aiden tell you how it all happened.

These scenes take place way back in book two, *Kiss Me*. Meaning Aiden had known the truth from the early morning hours of Sunday, September 25th until Saturday, December 17th when she finally told him. I think knowing this, you can now better understand his frustration with Keatyn, why he did the cute sex survey to learn about her past relationships, why he wanted to build a strong foundation together, why when he gave her the dirt he told her he didn't care if they had been lying to each other, and why he was making her wait.

To get you back into the story, we'll start with Keatyn's point of view from *Kiss Me*.

Friday, September 23rd

I WISH WE DIDN'T FIGHT.
12:55PM

KEATYN

GARRETT CALLS ME as I'm leaving lunch. I tell Dawson that I have to take a quick call and send him off to his next class. I'm freaking out a bit because Garrett never calls me. He always texts me and has me call him back.

"What's wrong?"

"Did you tell Vanessa where you are?"

"No."

"Keatyn, it's important that you tell me the truth. I won't yell at you if you did. I know this has been hard on you, but if you did, it's imperative that I know."

"I swear to you on my sisters' lives that I'm telling you the truth. What's going on?"

"Vanessa may be missing."

"Missing how?"

"She apparently posted something on Facebook about how she

talked to you. That you wanted everyone to know you were getting better."

"She just wants to act like she knows what's going on."

"Well, that may be, but she went to a club last night and RiAnne says no one has seen her since." He swallows loudly. "Vincent was at the same club."

"And you think something's happened to her? But you told me if I kept my friends in the dark they'd be safe. Did you lie to me? Do you think he's done something to her?"

"We don't know. We aren't running surveillance on him twenty-four-seven anymore."

I'm shocked. "Why not?!"

"I was told to cut back."

"By who?"

"James."

"Is it a money thing?"

"I think they were pretty surprised at how much the bill was, yes. But in their defense, it's been almost a month and we haven't produced any compelling results. The goal was to gather information that we could use against him. Other than him being at the same places as some of your friends, his going to Oregon, New York, and a few coincidental Facebook things, we have nothing. Nothing we could take to a judge, anyway."

"Do you think for my safety we should be watching him more?"

"I don't know that twenty-four-seven is the answer, but, yes, I'd like to have the freedom to do what we think is best. For example, my man followed him to the club, but then went off duty."

"From now on, you have the freedom to do what you think is best. Just bill me. And you need to give me more details about Vanessa because what you're saying doesn't make sense. Vanessa never went to a club alone. She made RiAnne and me go with her. And she may not have told RiAnne who she was leaving with, but she would have told her she was leaving. RiAnne was always her cover."

"What do you mean, her cover?"

"It's just not that unusual for her to go off with a guy for the weekend. And when she did that, she always told her dad that she was staying at RiAnnes. What did RiAnne say, exactly?"

"On her own wall, she said that Vanessa is missing, but on your Facebook wall she said, Vanessa is off radar and I'm going to be pissed if you two are having a reunion without me.

"Off radar means RiAnne has no idea where she is. You need to send her a message. Don't write on her wall. Send her a direct message. Tell her that Vanessa is not with me. That I haven't spoken to her or anyone else since my party. Tell her—and this is im-portant—that I pinkie swear. She'll come home, Garrett. She always does. I'm sure it's just a coincidence that he was there."

"Like it was just a coincidence that he was in New York at Brooklyn's tournament? I don't think so. When she comes home, Keatyn, I'd like her to come home alive. We can't find Vincent either."

"What do you mean?"

"We can't find him. He's not at home. Didn't go to his office today. His assistant said she wasn't sure when he'd be back."

"Wow," is all I manage to mutter out. My mind is going in a million directions. Trying to process it all.

"When she went off with guys before, did she go to the same place? Is there somewhere we can look for her?"

"Not really. She'd take off and come back with some amazing story. And pictures. Always pictures. Do you really think she could be with Vincent?"

"I don't believe in coincidences."

I remember her telling me that Vincent was hot that day at the hotel. "You might check The Chateau. It's her favorite hotel and it's where she met Vincent to begin with."

"I'll call you if I hear anything. You swear to me, she doesn't know where you are? If she does, I want you out of there now. I'm serious."

"I swear."

I hit the end button on my phone with a shaking hand. I know at any moment I'm going to burst into tears. I can't go to class.

I run my hand through my hair, look up, and see the chapel at the top of the hill. I put my head down and quickly walk toward it.

The heavy wooden doors open with a creak. Thankfully, no one is here. I choose a pew in the back row and plop down. I fold my hands and say a prayer.

Please, God, let Vanessa be okay. I don't understand this. I gave up everything. My friends. My family. My home. I wanted to put as much distance as I could between us. I did it because I thought it would keep them safe. They told me it would keep them safe. I was so sure of my decision when I made it. I can still see the photo of the girls. I can still hear the voice in my head that told me they'd be safe. I don't want anyone hurt because of me, and they are really the ones I did this for. They are the ones I gave my life up for. And I'll give it up forever as long as those four little smiles stay safe.

Tears stream down my face as I'm praying, but when I think about the girls, I start bawling. I just put my face in my hands and cry. I miss them so much.

A hand touches my knee and a silky voice says, "Boots."

I look up and Aiden's eyes meet my tear-filled ones. Those green

9

eyes that see straight through me. Those green eyes that always make me feel emotionally naked.

I close my eyes and start crying again. I don't know why he's here. He's supposed to be mad at me. But he doesn't act like he's mad anymore. He wraps his arms around me and I melt into his chest.

Friday, September 23rd

I WISH WE DIDN'T FIGHT.
12:55PM

AIDEN

THERE'S SOMETHING ABOUT the stillness of the chapel and the tears falling in black-mascara tracks down her beautiful face that make me stop in realization.

This girl is more than just a trophy to me. More than just a prize to be won and paraded around school on my arm. More than just a girl I want to get out of her plaid skirt.

She could be *the* girl.

The one I wished for that night.

The girl I never want to cry. The girl who puts a smile on my face even when she pisses me off.

With most girls, all I want to know is *your room or mine?*

I want to know everything about Keatyn. I want to meet her family, see her baby pictures, hear stories about her growing up. I want to know what makes her happy, what makes her sad, and if it's in my power, I don't want her to ever be sad.

I want her to have a life filled with love and happiness—and me.

That's the truth. I'm in love with her.

Probably have been since she rushed down the hill, stole the soccer ball—with her dress and golden hair flying behind her, looking like a goddess—dribbled down the field, and kicked it right past me.

What girl does that?

What *new* girl does that?

But when she smirked at me, I saw more than beauty and challenge. I saw myself reflected in her unusual purple-blue eyes. I felt my soul awaken—my heart kick-started.

You hear about love at first sight, but never really believe in it. Never expect it will happen to you. Most of what I have experienced up until now falls into the lust-at-first-sight category. She just feels different. She has brought out a range of emotions in me I didn't realize I had.

The level of anger, jealousy, and rage she makes me feel drives me nuts.

But there's more.

Desire and love mixed with a fierce need to protect her and to care for her.

I want to know what makes her tick, and what's happened in her life to make her what she is today. She eludes confidence, but there's something behind the curtain—just below the surface, is it sorrow? Or is she just homesick?

She closes her eyes and starts crying again.

I wrap my arms around her, causing her to practically melt into my chest. I try to soothe her by whispering in her ear. "Shhhh, it'll be okay."

Her body shudders, and she sobs a bit more. I slide my hand into her silky hair, causing the sweet scent of cotton candy to permeate my senses as I hold her tightly. I can hear her heartbeat against my chest. I swear, it feels like it beats for me.

"Why aren't you in class?" she whispers.

I run my hand through her hair again, trying to calm her. "I saw you sitting on the bench, talking on your phone. You had your head down the whole time. I was waiting so I could apologize for last night. Again. It feels like I'm always apologizing to you. But when you looked up, I could tell by the look on your face that something was wrong. And when you marched straight to the chapel, I knew you must be really upset. What happened?"

"I got some bad news from my family. Um, my friend, she has this guy who has been stalking her. She's maybe missing right now."

"And they think the stalker might have hurt her? What was their relationship? Did they date?"

"No, they think it started when he saw a picture of her."

"A picture?"

"Yeah. Um, my friend wanted to be an actress, and he saw a picture of her. They met. He flirted with her. Told her he wanted to make a movie with her. They actually had become friends. She thought he was nice. Until he tried to kidnap her."

She's telling me how all of this happened to her friend, but her hands are shaking, and the tears continue to fall. Why does it feel like she's talking about herself? Why do I feel like there's more to the story?

A lot more.

I try to make some sense of it. "So why isn't the guy in jail?"

"She invited him to a party. There was a commotion. He told

her he was taking her to a van out back. But she got away. A guy fought with him. The police came. They took her statement. She was hysterical. Threw up. She'd been drinking. It was her word against his. There was just not enough evidence."

"That's awful," I say softly, pulling her back against my chest. "Tell me the rest."

And she does. About how her friend's family sent her away. How Keatyn can't see her again. How they think this stalker is still after her friend. It's crazy. And scary.

"I'm sure she'll be okay. Is that why you came here? To pray?"

She nods her head. "Yes. And I knew if I went to class I would start crying. I wouldn't want anyone to see me like this. I'm sure I look gross." She hangs her head in shame.

I gently push her chin up. "I told you before. I doubt you're ever gross." Seriously, I've never seen someone look so beautiful when they cry. My sister's face always turns bright red, her eyes get glassy, and her nose runs.

Keatyn delicately slides her finger across her cheek to wipe the mascara off her face as she turns to me. "Aiden, do you ever lie?"

"I don't like to be lied to, so I try not to," I reply, focusing more on the way she says my name. How it makes me stir in places I shouldn't right now. She's upset. Sex is the last thing that should be on my mind. But it's there. God, it's there. I can control myself around girls, but with her, it's a constant struggle.

"My friend. She was afraid, so she left town. Just up and left. Didn't tell very many people where she went. She's living somewhere else under a different name. She's meeting new people and making new friends, but she hasn't told them what happened. Or that she's using a new name. She feels like she's living a lie."

"Is she just lying about her name?"

"No, she has to lie about her past, too. She wasn't famous, but her parents are. People would recognize her name."

"Well, I'm sure her new friends would understand if they found out."

She smiles, lies down and puts her head in my lap, then pulls her feet up onto the pew and curls up in a ball. "I'm afraid for her."

When she speaks those words, a chill runs through me. But not because of her friend. I'm afraid for Keatyn—because she's afraid. And I can't shake the feeling that there's something she's not telling me.

I push her soft hair back off her face gently and run my hand across her cheek. She needs reassurance. And I want to be the one who kisses it and makes it better. "What I told you in class. Whenever you need me, I'm there. I know we were talking about tutoring, but it goes for everything. You can always come talk to me when you're upset."

She lets out a big sigh as fresh tears fall down her face. "No, I can't. Half the time you're mad at me. You got so mad at me last night. I really wish we didn't fight, Aiden."

"It bothers you?" Thank God.

"Yes, it bothers me. I like you. I wish we could be friends."

"You know why I get mad, don't you?" Because I'm jealous as hell.

"Yes. You jump to conclusions about things that you shouldn't." Wrong. "Half the time you don't let me finish my sentence before you go storming off." True, because she drives me nuts. "And then you pretend punch my head." This makes me smile.

I bend down to kiss her forehead. "I'm sorry. I promise not to pretend punch your head ever again."

"Thank you."

My cell buzzes again, causing me to glance at it. "It's my sister. She's called me four times. Hang on."

When I answer, Peyton goes, "Aiden! Where are you? Are you with Keatyn? Do you know what time it is?"

"Yeah," I reply. "I didn't realize it was that late. It's fine. Don't worry. And yes, she's with me."

"I don't know what you are doing, but you both better get your asses to the field house. Now."

I end the call, not needing to hear anymore.

"Are we in trouble for skipping French?" Keatyn asks.

"We didn't just skip French, Boots. School's out. You're supposed to be in the dance locker room, and I'm supposed to be getting ready for the game."

She sits up quickly. "What time is it?"

"5:45."

"Ohmigosh! Are we going to be in trouble?"

The defeat in her face is like a blow to my gut. She doesn't need more trouble. She's been through enough today. And, maybe, she's been through enough before she ever got here. I need to fix this for her.

"Tell you what. I'll go talk to the Dean. You go get ready for dance."

She attempts to clean up her face and straightens her sexy, red dance skirt. Her hair is damp around her face and causes her tendrils to curl a little. I give her a smile, then hold open the chapel door for her as she takes off running toward the field house.

FLAVOR OF THE WEEK.
6:15PM

"YOU NEED TO get to the locker room, son," the Dean says after I explain what happened to Keatyn—how she got some bad news from home, how I saw her get a phone call and then go directly to the chapel, how upset she was, and why I hope she won't be in trouble.

"Thank you, sir," I say, knowing we won't get any demerits or detentions.

"And, we need a win tonight," he adds.

I leave the Dean's office happy that at least Keatyn will have one less thing to worry about. I rush into the locker room, throwing on my pads and getting suited up.

"Nice of you to join us, Arrington," Coach says, but thankfully he doesn't press the subject. Probably because I'm never late, and he knows I must have a good reason for being so today.

But, unfortunately not everyone feels that way.

Dawson gives me shit the second he's out of earshot. "What's going on with you and Keatyn?"

"Nothing."

"Bullshit. Tell me where you were all afternoon."

"In the chapel."

Dawson is all pumped up and mad. His hands are closed in tight fists, and he's dying to take a swing at me.

"Get your head in the game, Dawson," Jake says, stepping between us. "You two can duke it out *after* we win."

But Dawson doesn't back down. He gets in my face. "If you were hooking up with my girl, you better hope the game never ends."

17

I don't bother to tell him that regardless of what he thinks Keatyn is *not* his girl.

Because if she truly loved him, when she was upset, she would have gone to him. She would have told *him* everything, not me.

But the second it crosses my mind, I realize that's not true. Because I know she didn't tell me everything.

My thoughts are interrupted by the Coach yelling at the team. "Let's get out there and win this one!"

I FOCUS ON the football game when I'm out on the field, but when I'm on the sidelines I watch Keatyn. She's off—messing up her dances.

I study her face from across the field. She looks stressed out. Preoccupied. Obviously, thinking about her friend.

She's not even really watching the game. Her eyes are constantly darting across the crowd—like she is trying to find someone she knows?

Or could she be in danger here?

"Arrington!" Coach yells out, calling for my attention. "You think you can make a fifty-yarder?"

"Yeah, sure," I reply confidently. "I do it in practice all the time."

"Then go do it!"

I run out onto the field and line up for the field goal—smiling as I think about getting a few more *Points for Dances*—and drill the ball through the goal posts.

For her.

Only for her.

AS THE TEAM makes our big entrance back onto the field after halftime, I hang to the back of the pack. The cheerleaders and dance team always line up for our return, and I need to talk to her.

She's shaking her pompoms but seemingly lost in thought when I stop directly in front of her and slide my hands down her arms. "Have you heard anything?"

She looks shocked that I stopped in the middle of the field to talk to her. It makes me wonder what kind of guys she's dated in the past. Is she not used to someone caring about her?

She gazes into my eyes and shakes her head. Her eyes are like windows into her soul. That bluish purple color makes me forget where I am.

I lean my helmet against her forehead, needing to be closer to her. "It'll be okay. I promise."

Then I take off running to catch up with the rest of the team before Coach yells at me.

Coach doesn't seem to have noticed my stopping, but Dawson sure did.

He grabs me by the face mask, pissed. "I told you to stay the hell away from her!"

"I can talk to whoever I want," I reply, shoving him away, standing up straighter, and preparing myself for a fight.

Dawson lunges toward me, but someone steps in between us.

"I told you, deal with this shit later," Jake yells at Dawson. "We've got a game to win. Focus on that."

"I don't give a shit," Dawson yells, but Jake drags him over to the bench.

"What's going on with you and Keatyn, anyway?" Logan asks, sliding up next to me. "You ditched all your afternoon classes and were with her? I'm all for you getting some tail, bro, but you can get kicked out for that shit. Not to mention, Dawson wants to pummel you. I'd hate to see my best friend shipped back to California over some freaking girl."

"It's not like that," I mutter as I run out onto the field for the start of the third quarter, praying that what I told Keatyn will come true. That it *will* all be okay.

AFTER THE GAME, I take a quick shower, hoping to be able to talk to Keatyn before she leaves for the weekend. She's going with my sister, Whitney, Dawson, and the rest of the popular crew to some spa up north.

What I'd really like to do is talk her out of going, but that probably won't happen. I know she's been looking forward to it.

Would it be bad of me to use her concern for her friend as a reason to stay?

Here.

With me.

As I'm leaving the field house, I notice her slip behind the bushes not far from the door. I'm going to say something witty, but then I see Dawson get into a limo with Whitney and Rachel and leave.

Why did they leave without her?

Did she decide not to go? Is that why she's hiding? She didn't want them to see her?

Wait, did she and Dawson break up?

I want to jump for joy and then kiss her, but her body language changes. Her shoulders slump forward in defeat, and I realize she's not happy about whatever just transpired.

"Why are we hiding in the bushes?" I whisper. "And why did they just leave without you?"

As she turns around, her chest brushes across mine—the unmistakable jolt of energy I know we both feel every time we touch causing her to hop backwards and almost fall into the bushes. I reach out and grab her, holding her upright.

Tears fill her gorgeous eyes.

"Whitney told me right before the game was over that even though I was sitting there when she asked, I wasn't invited. Then she said something nasty about me being Dawson's flavor of the week and how he's going to hook up with Rachel. I was going to cancel on him anyway. I have a car coming to pick me up in the morning, and then I'm going to New York. I guess Dawson is still mad at me about today. Or maybe Whitney is right, and I am just the flavor of the week."

I listen to her every word, thrilled that she's standing here in my arms, but mad that my sister and her friends could be so mean.

"You know, you're even beautiful when you cry," I say, brushing a few tears from her cheek.

"If this is the new and improved Aiden, I like him better already. I just don't get why Dawson would leave. He bought me a key-to-his-heart necklace a while ago. He says he really likes me. But then he does this? Just leaves? Is that what they do, Aiden? Is this just a game to them?"

"It all seems kind of odd, especially after what Dawson said to me at halftime."

"He got mad you stopped to check on me, didn't he?"

"Yeah, he was really pissed."

"It was nice of you. I'm pretty much exhausted. I can't wait to go to sleep."

I move us out of the bushes and walk her to her dorm. I want to invite her to mine. I don't want her to be alone.

But her body language is telling me otherwise. If she's like my sister, she probably wants to go cry in private. The girl has had a rough day—first her friend and now this.

But I want her to know I'm here for her. Always.

I give her a kiss on the cheek. "If you hear anything about your friend, let me know, okay?"

"Okay. Night, Aiden."

"Night, Boots," I say with a smirk, then pat her on the back—a redo of the end of our twenty-nine dances night.

"Very funny," she says as she walks into her dorm.

But at least I made her smile.

I'D KICK HIS ASS.
11:30PM

I GO TO my dorm and flip on the twinkle lights I put up for her—feeling hopeful. She and Dawson will be over after this, and I want to ask her to Homecoming—this weekend while Dawson is gone. I just need to figure out the perfect way.

I close my eyes and run through all the ways I've seen girls get asked over the years, but none of them are right. My train of thought switches to how vulnerable she looked today in the chapel.

How she practically curled up into my lap.

How she turns me on.

My phone rings, startling me. When I see it's her, I feel like I just got caught. That she knows I'm thinking about her.

"Is your friend okay?" I ask.

"Yes. I just got good news."

"I'm glad. I've been praying for that all day."

"Me too. Thanks for today, Aiden. For talking—well, for listening to me and for getting us out of trouble for skipping."

A Facebook notification dings in my ear. I move my phone in front of my face to see it. Whitney has posted a photo of Dawson kissing Rachel's cheek in the limo.

"Wow. That hurts," she says.

"What hurts?" I ask, hoping she didn't just see it.

"Whitney just posted a photo of Dawson kissing Rachel."

"Only on the cheek. I just saw."

She starts to cry again then chokes out, "I have to go, Aiden."

"Wait," I say, but it's too late. She's already hung up on me.

Shit.

My instant reaction is to want to fix everything for her, and since I can't change what's going on with her friend, I'm only left with one choice. Because no matter how much I want her and Dawson to be over, I can't stand to see her hurt. And I'm pretty sure I'm the only one she told about what happened.

I get up and go bang on Riley's door.

"What's up?" he asks. "We going to sneak in Bryce's room while he's gone, hook up with random hot girls, and drink all his stash?"

"Have you talked to your brother?" I ask.

"I saw he was being a dick to you at the game tonight. I'm sorry."

"I can handle it. That's not why I asked though. He left with everyone for the weekend, without Keatyn."

"Why? Are they in a fight because of today? Where is she?"

"I'm pretty sure she's in her room crying."

"So what did he say to her?"

"That's just it, he didn't say anything. But before the game was over, Whitney told Keatyn that even though she was sitting at the lunch table when she asked, Keatyn wasn't invited. She told her she is Dawson's flavor of the week. That he has been texting Rachel and that they are going to hook up. She was standing in the bushes watching them leave. And she was crying, Riley. It kills me when she cries."

"What is it about her? Even though she's dating my brother, I'd kick his ass if he hurt her."

"You guys are good friends."

"Yeah, but it's more than that. She's strong and fierce, but it's like there's something behind it, something that brings out the protector in me."

"Like when you slammed me against the locker for talking shit about her?"

"Yeah, exactly like that."

"Maybe you can do that again," I suggest. "Find out if Dawson is aware of what Whitney did."

"Are you sure that's what you want?" Riley asks. "I know you like her. You could spend all weekend alone with her. She's got to be pissed at my brother. You could sneak in, steal her away."

I shake my head. "I couldn't live with myself. She's hurt, Riley, and we need to fix it. Even if that means she ends up with Dawson."

Riley appraises me. I'm not sure, but I think what I just said earned me some respect with him.

"And I'm sick of Whitney pulling this kind of crap," he says. "I'm calling Dawson, now."

"Wait. Why don't you call Jake instead? Find out the truth.

Was it Dawson's idea to leave her because he wants to hook up with Rachel, or did Whitney manipulate things to keep Dawson and Keatyn apart?"

While he grabs his cell and makes the call, I sit on his bed, still wondering what I'm doing.

Any other girl, and I'd be taking advantage of the situation, consoling her—with my dick.

But I don't want Keatyn by default.

Because I'm pretty sure I'm in love with her.

I must be.

I'm behaving like an idiot.

On the other hand, it's not like Dawson will come all the way back here on his own.

Maybe I can do the right thing and still reap the rewards.

Riley hangs up and says to me, "Dawson and Jake are pissed! I'm going to pick them up. You want to come?"

Or not.

Shit.

"Uh, naw. You go ahead."

I go back to my room, lie in my bed, kick myself for telling, and fall asleep wondering why everything I do concerning her never seems to work out right.

Saturday, September 24th
JUST IN TIME.
8:20AM

I'M GOING TO workout when I run into Jake.

"You're back, huh?"

"Yeah, just in time, too," he says.

"For what?"

"For Dawson and Keatyn to make up."

I swallow hard. "They made up?"

"Yeah, she was getting in the cab ready to leave right when we pulled up. She was pissed at first, but he totally sweet talked her into letting him go with her."

Now I feel sick. "Uh, that's great for them," I say, forcing a smile.

When I get down to the gym, I head straight for the punching bag and totally pretend the bag is Dawson's face.

But once I get some of my frustrations out, I realize that's it is all my fault, and I should probably be punching myself.

I WORK OUT and then go get pizza with Logan and some of the guys. We hang out at the sports bar for awhile, watching college football on their multiple screens.

While we're there, Logan leans over and says, "What's up your butt today?"

"I'm an idiot."

"Dallas told me it was because of you that Dawson found out what Whitney did. If you like Keatyn, why the hell did you do that?"

"Because I'm an idiot," I repeat.

"Well, they're together now. Not much you can do about it." He slaps me on the back. "Dude, we're getting you laid tonight. It's been all semester. No wonder you're being an idiot. You can't think when your balls are blue."

"That's bullshit, and you know it. If I recall, you went for months without doing it before and after Maggie."

"Shut up. That's different. I loved her." He studies me then says, "Shit. Do you love her?"

I rub my hands down my face in frustration. "Pretty sure."

"You thought you loved Chelsea last year. Look how that turned out. I thought I loved Maggie. That went to shit. We're too young to worry about love. We need to hook up, get off, and move on to the next one. We can worry about all that love shit once we're done with college. Until then, we're going to have some fun."

I try to focus on the games, but I can't stop thinking about what Keatyn's doing—hopefully it's not Dawson.

I remind myself that she intended to shop. Maybe that's all they will do. Shop. And be so tired afterwards they just go to sleep.

But I doubt it.

Everyone says they've already done it. I'm pretty sure they did it that weekend in the Hamptons when she was mad at her ex.

I screwed up by behaving like a jealous idiot when she told me about her ex. Then Logan told me that girls weren't worth the hassle. And after what happened last year at Prom, I had to agree with him.

But I was wrong. She's worth the hassle.

WHEN I GET back to my dorm, her being with Dawson isn't the only thing on my mind. It's the underlying feeling I have about our conversation in the chapel.

That what she was saying was more about her than her friend.

I can't talk to my friends about it. So I call my parents, who put me on speaker like they always do.

After our initial greeting, chatting about the weather, their travels, and football, talk turns to my classes.

"How are your grades so far?" Mom asks.

"Actually, pretty good. I got a C plus on my last French test."

"Really?" Dad asks. "That's great. We heard from your sister that you have a crush on your tutor. That the reason for the improvement?"

"Probably," I say. "Actually, that's part of why I called. I need your advice."

"What about?" Mom asks.

"There's something going on in her personal life. She told me a little bit about it, but I know there's stuff she's not telling me. I want her to confide in me. Trust me. How can I make her?"

"You can't *make* her trust you, son," Dad says. "You have to *earn* her trust if you want her to confide in you."

"What did Peyton tell you about her?"

"Not much. Just that you like her, but she likes someone

else," Dad says.

"That's not all," Mom contradicts. "I heard she's on the dance team as well as Varsity soccer. Peyton said she's really pretty, really nice, and a breath of fresh air at the school. It sounds like there has been some tension between her and Whitney this semester."

"That's because Whitney can be mean." I tell them about how Keatyn is seeing Dawson, how Whitney hates it, and what she did last night.

"But I thought Whitney broke up with Dawson last year?" Mom asks.

"She did. But since he's gotten more serious with Keatyn, it's making her mad. I don't know that she really likes Dawson, it's the attention they get as a couple that I think she's jealous of."

"High school drama," Dad laughs.

"It's more than that," I say with a sigh. "I really like her. She's just . . . different. Special. Yeah, she's gorgeous, but it's more. It's like—this sounds crazy—she's supposed to be with me." I spill my guts and tell them everything that's happened between us—starting from when she kicked the soccer ball at my face to last night. I take a big breath then say, "And I screwed up again last night. She was upset. I didn't want her to be hurt, so I told Riley what happened and then he called Jake who told Dawson and then they came back. I was hoping to get some time alone with her this weekend and ask her to Homecoming. Instead, she took Dawson to New York City with her."

"You've never had a problem getting girls to like you," Mom says.

"Usually too many do," Dad chuckles.

"What's wrong with her?" Mom asks. "You're practically

perfect. And so adorable."

I roll my eyes. "You're my mom. You have to say that. And there's nothing's wrong with her. She's perfect."

"Are her and Dawson going steady?"

"No one goes steady anymore, Mom. They're in a relationship. They go out."

"Same thing. Are they?"

"No."

"Then if you want to take her to the dance, you should ask her," Mom suggests. "The worst thing that can happen is she could say no. You just have to be the guy who asks first."

"You think?"

"Well, if he hasn't asked her, there's no reason why you can't. Do it when she gets back."

I consider it. I will be devastated if she says no.

But I also know she's worth the risk. "You're right. I'll do it. I'll ask her on Monday after school when we meet up to study."

"Thataboy," Dad says.

"Good luck," Mom says. "Love you."

"Bye. Love you guys, too."

Before the call ends, I hear Dad chuckle and say to Mom, "Sounds like he's got it bad."

I hang up thinking Dad's right.

I do.

A BOTTLE OF BOOZE.
11:45PM

LOGAN AND I are at the Cave, sitting on a log around the fire.

He's in a shitty mood because Maggie is flirting with someone. I'm pretty sure she does it just to make him jealous, but I can't say that. He'd get pissed at me, too.

So I do the next best thing. I point over to a group of cheerleaders, most of whom are drunk.

"Alicia keeps looking at you," I tell him, hoping to cheer him up as I pass him a bottle of booze.

He glances in her direction. "She's got a great rack. Not much between the ears, though."

"That's not true," I say. "She was in math with me last year and got straight A's. I think she's really smart, just lacks common sense."

"Hmm," Logan says, a smile finally appearing on his face. "Let's go over there."

The girls who are left here don't have boyfriends. If they did, they'd be off hooking up somewhere. Alicia touches Logan's arm and says in a high-pitched tone, "I couldn't believe the amazing catch you made in the game last night."

Logan passes her the bottle and smiles.

That's pretty much all it takes.

Her best friend, Ashley, flirts with me. First complimenting the personal-best field goal I made and then complimenting my biceps. I'm fine with her flirting with me. At least until Logan and Alicia decide to leave together—or at least start making out. I'm trying to be a good wingman.

To not think about how much today sucked. About how all I could think about is what Dawson and Keatyn are doing.

And it kinda makes me feel sick. I should have offered to go with her. I should have suggested we leave that night. It seems like that's how most of our relationship has gone—me doing something stupid and later kicking myself for it.

I smile, thinking about her kicking the soccer ball at me and how I call her Boots because of it.

Ashley takes my smile as flirting, because now she's caressing the bicep she was admiring.

My parents are right, though. If Dawson doesn't ask her this weekend, I'm going to ask Monday night at tutoring.

I just don't know how.

I look up at the stars and wonder if she's looking at them right now, too.

Probably not. They're probably in bed.

I snatch the bottle out of Alicia's hand and take a long slug.

"My turn," Ashley says, taking a slug of her own. "So, Aiden." She slides closer to me. "I heard you don't have a date for Homecoming yet. You planning to ask anyone?"

"Probably," I reply noncommittally.

She hands the bottle off to someone and rests her hands on my hips. "Wanna go for a walk?"

A walk isn't really what she wants. I know exactly what will happen if I agree. We'll go to the lacrosse field and hook up—like we have before.

And I want to hook up.

Just not with her.

Part of me wonders what would happen if I did. If Keatyn would hear about it. If it would make her jealous. But jealousy would imply that she actually likes me.

Although most of the time she acts like she doesn't, I know differently.

In the chapel, she seemed so fragile. So sweet. And the way she clung to me—

"Aiden!" Ashley says. "I asked you a question."

"Um, I'm not feeling great. Maybe some other time," I say, not wanting to hurt her feelings. When did I start to care? In the past, I wouldn't have said that. I would have just told her I wasn't interested. Actually, that's a lie. I would have taken her somewhere to hook up. But that was before Keatyn. Somehow, she's changed me.

"But—" she says as I give Logan a quick salute and get the hell out of there.

On the way back to my room, I run into Chelsea coming out of the boys' dorm.

"Hey, Aiden. All alone?" I roll my eyes and don't bother to reply. As I walk past her, she grabs my arm. "I was talking to you."

"Yeah, well, I don't have anything to say."

"You miss me," she says. "We were good together."

"You were screwing around on me. Somehow, that doesn't constitute *good.*"

She leans in and tries to kiss me. I dodge her. "Don't."

"I'm sorry, okay. I'm sorry about Prom night. I was drunk." She gives me a sweet smile. "I think we should try again, Triple A. Let's go to your room. I'll make it up to you."

I hesitate for a second, because it was good. And I really thought I liked her. But then she humiliated me.

Chelsea responds to my hesitation by placing her lips on mine and shoving her tongue in my mouth.

I push her off me. "Stop it. You're coming out of the dorm. I'm not into sloppy seconds."

"That's not what I hear."

"What do you mean by that?"

"You and Dawson are both doing the new girl. I heard they're together this weekend. Probably doing all sorts of fun, naughty things. I mean, Dawson is fine."

"I'm not doing the new girl," I tell her, backing away further. "It's not like that."

"You haven't hooked up with her?" Her eyes widen. "Wait. Do you really like her? Like you did me. When you like a girl you make her wait."

"I didn't make you wait. We'd been together all of two weeks. I just thought—"

"I was into you."

"Well, you certainly acted like it. We'd done everything but had sex."

"So we did some stuff. Big deal. And you have no room to talk. You had been with plenty of girls. You asked me to Prom, not to be your girlfriend. I assumed you were still having fun, too."

"It really doesn't matter anymore, Chelsea. I don't care."

She pushes me against the wall and slides her hand down my chest. "I'm just going to say it. I want you, A. Tonight. Now. Tomorrow. Let's go to Homecoming together. Rewrite our fate."

"Sorta like fate," I mutter.

"Exactly," she says, bringing her lips to mine.

I put my hand in front of my mouth to block her kiss, not wanting her to ruin my lips again.

"Not interested, Chelsea," I say, then turn to go up to my room.

I shut the door in her face when she follows me, but from outside the door she says, "All you'll ever be is Keatyn's sloppy seconds, Aiden. You should forget about her and be with me."

I don't bother to reply, but as I flop on my bed, I can't help wonder if she's right.

I TRY TO go to sleep, but my brain won't stop running through my past with Chelsea.

Logan and Maggie were going to Prom together. They were happy and in love. It was all mushy and gooey, and something I hadn't yet experienced. I thought Chelsea was hot, so I asked her to Prom one night at the Cave. She said yes, and things were intense between us for the two weeks before.

I thought it was love.

I don't think I really loved her. I think I wanted to *be* in love. To experience more than just the rush of hooking up. To have someone who cared about me for more than just what I did on the soccer field or the way I looked. Which is completely hypocritical, because I thought I was in love with Chelsea for two reasons. She looked sexy in her little cheerleading outfit, and she gave great head. Probably not the makings of a fairytale love.

I remember being so embarrassed of myself, my actions. Getting drunk, ruining Logan and Maggie's night, getting it on with not one, but two girls.

And then I made that damn wish on the moon.

For my perfect girl.

I get off my bed and gaze out my window at it.

I know I got my wish. I know Keatyn is my perfect girl. I just thought when that girl came into my life it would be easy and effortless.

Then I start thinking about what she told me in the chapel yesterday. Replaying it all. Her friend being stalked. Almost kidnapped at her party. How her friend just up and left and didn't tell very many people. How she's living under a different name. How her parents are famous. How she feels like she's living a lie.

The more I think about it, the more certain I am. She was talking about herself.

So who is she?

I shut my blackout curtains, turn on the lamp over my bed, grab my laptop, and start searching.

I start with her name, *Keatyn Monroe*. But all I really get from that is a bunch of Marilyn Monroe. I go through pages and pages of searches, but can't find anything.

I switch to an image search, still nothing.

So I try Facebook.

None of the Keatyn Monroes are her.

Then I search her name and the word *stalker*.

Nothing.

But wait, she said her friend is lying about who she is. Could she have changed her name?

Or maybe just her last name?

I search just *Keatyn*.

Then switch to *Keatyn* on Facebook.

I search through hundreds of profiles, not finding her.

I stand up and pace the room.

What do I know about her? *She lived in California. Famous parents.*

Famous and California, could her parents be actors? Involved with Hollywood? Or maybe a professional athlete? Or run a company people would know of?

I look at the clock and sigh. It's nearly four in the morning. This is ridiculous.

I've been searching for way too long.

Clearly, I am obsessed.

But, at the same time, I feel a little bit invigorated. Like I'm getting closer.

I search the name *Keatyn* along with the words *famous parents*. I get a lot of hits about current actors with famous parents, but still not what I'm looking for.

What do people in Hollywood do? Where do they go? Move premieres, right?

I type in *Keatyn, Movie Premiere* using the image search function.

I scroll through a few pages, my vision starting to blur.

I'll look through these and then stop for the night.

On page ten, my eyes move across the screen in a haze then stop.

Wait. What was that?

I go back a few pictures and spot a photo that could be her.

I click to make it bigger.

It's a photo from a popular kid's award show. I immediately recognize the actress Abby Johnston. And standing next to her is *Keatyn Douglas, daughter of the late Mark Douglas.*

Wow. I was right.

I can't help but smile. She's about twelve in the photo, not as tall as her mom. Her face is still chubby with baby fat, not the chiseled cheekbones she has today. Her hair is long and blonde, she's tan, and wearing just a little mascara. She and her mom share the same smile, and she's adorable.

I do a quick search to pull up Mark Douglas. See he was a professional model. And that she has her father's eyes.

I stop, get up to stretch my legs again, and grab a Mountain

Dew and a bag of chips. I need caffeine and food.

After chugging about half the can and shoving chips into my mouth, I switch to Facebook and easily find Keatyn Douglas. There's a photo of her and a guy. I click on it and read her description. *Me and B in Monaco. <3*

I scroll through her other photos. Her and the guy, who's real name is Brooklyn Wright, looking in love. On the beach. Surfing. Kissing. Getting matching tattoos. Her with her *BFFs, Vanessa and RiAnne.* Her prom night, looking gorgeous in a sparkly gown with a handsome guy who looks sort of familiar. Then some photos of her with another guy named Cush.

I close my eyes, feeling like a stalker. Feeling like I'm invading her personal life.

But at the same time, I need to know.

I click on the album titled *Birthday Party.* She's looking exceptionally hot, wearing a little strapless cream dress with a flouncy skirt, her long legs tan and her feet encased in gorgeous heels with jewels on them. She's wearing a simple gold heart locket, the one she wears every day. I notice the date. *Saturday, August 20th.*

I glance at my calendar. Her first day here was Thursday, August 25th. Orientation day. The day she kicked the soccer ball at me. Only five days after her party. I remember what she told me in the chapel. *She invited him to a party. There was a commotion. He told her he was taking her to a van out back. But she got away. A guy fought with him. The police came. They took her statement. She was hysterical. Threw up. She'd been drinking. It was her word against his. There was just not enough evidence.*

I click out of her photos and take a look at her wall.

There is a post yesterday morning from RiAnne. It says, *I miss you.*

I scroll back some more. See the talk about her. The gossip. The rumors. She is the one who left. She's the one lying about who she is. She's the one who almost got kidnapped. That's why she was so upset today. Why she was shaking.

She said only a few people know she left.

And one of those people has to be Brooklyn Wright. I've seen their texts. That means she trusts him. Were they two people pulled apart by circumstances beyond their control?

Does she still love him?

That question hurts to think about. Literally hurts my heart. But, yet, she's with Dawson. So he can't be that special. Can he?

The more important question, though, is what am I going to do?

Should I confront her?

I'm afraid for her. Those words gave me a chill in the chapel, and they do the same to me now. I can't confront her. She's in trouble. She said she feels like she's living a lie. This isn't easy for her. I think about what she must be going through. She's almost kidnapped at her birthday party. Five days later, she's forced to not only leave all her friends, but have no contact with them. She was forced to leave her boyfriend, the surfer. She was sent to Eastbrooke. It's no wonder she got so upset when I quoted Keats. It's no wonder things are up in the air with them.

Although sometimes, like in the chapel, it feels like me and Keatyn are close, I know now that we aren't. I need to get to know her better. I need to find out what's in her heart. What's in her soul. And not just think about getting in her pants. In fact, I'm going to make a vow to myself right now. I'm going to take things slow with her. Be her friend. I don't want our relationship—whatever that turns out to be—based on anything other than trust.

I really wish we didn't fight, Aiden.

And I'm going to stop pushing for it to happen.

Because I don't want to fight either.

I close my laptop, then peek through my curtains at the moon again. It's a brilliant night, the sky full of stars.

I shut the curtains and turn off my lamp, leaving the twinkle lights on. As I lie in bed, I suddenly know how I'll ask her to Homecoming. I want to give her the moon and the stars.

Sunday, September 25th
QUITE LIMBER.
10AM

LOGAN AND I grab a smoothie then go down to the gym to work out. It's fairly early on Sunday morning and pretty quiet.

"So, how'd last night go?" he asks as he adds more weight to the barbell I'm getting ready to bench press. "You and Ashley hook up?"

"What about you?" I ask, avoiding the question and hoping to distract him.

"Yeah. Get this, we did it in the stairwell of her dorm. That was a first."

"You could have gotten caught."

"I know, but that's what made it all the more exciting. Plus the railings," he says as I grunt, pushing the weight upward.

"Good job," he says, spotting for me. "You want more weight?"

"No, this is hard enough," I laugh. "So back to the railings."

"She's a cheerleader. A gymnast. Quite limber," he says with a smirk. "Use your imagination. My ass was warm while yours was probably freezing on the lacrosse bleachers . . ." He stops mid-sentence.

I do another rep then sit up and see the reason for the interruption. At one end of the weight room is a glass-enclosed yoga room. Maggie just walked in, rolled out a yoga mat, and started her workout by putting her hands above her head almost as if in prayer, then she switches to a different position. I don't know the name of the yoga poses, but apparently Logan does.

"Downward dog," he says with a sigh. "Gotta love yoga."

"Probably because she's not wearing much," I agree.

"I know, those skimpy spandex shorts, the bra top. She has her hair in a braid just like the first time we kissed—" He moves quickly, hurt in his eyes. "My turn," he says. "Give me twenty over my personal best."

"Logan, why don't you go do some yoga instead? Talk to her."

"One. She hates me. Two. She probably already knows I was with Alicia. Nothing is private here. And three. She hates me."

"Maybe you should ask her to Homecoming," I suggest. His eyes linger on Maggie, making me feel bad for him. It's obvious that he still loves her. "I don't understand why you won't talk to her."

"We do talk."

"I mean about your relationship. You like her. Fix it."

"No thanks. I'll take messy drunken stairway sex over having my heart stomped on again, thank you very much. Now, be a good spotter and add more weight." When he notices she's looking in our direction, he flexes in the mirror, popping out the back muscles that all the girls seem to love. Then he lies down and benches a new personal best—which means he gets to ring the bell.

"You're totally showing off for her," I tease.

"Shut up," he replies as he runs over to the big bell close to the yoga room and rings it loudly.

AFTER OUR WORKOUT, we head back to the dorm.

"You want to go into town for lunch? Chinese, maybe?"

"No, I can't. I have some stuff to do."

"Homework sucks," he says.

I nod, even though that's not what I'm talking about.

I shower, get dressed, then drive into the city and hit numerous stores before I have everything I need.

When I get back to my dorm, I set up the ladder I borrowed from the janitor and lock my door.

I don't want anyone to see what I'm doing.

I want her to be the first to see it.

TWO HOURS LATER, I lie back on the bed and decide it looks like shit.

She's going to hate it.

Hell, I hate it.

I can't even make out the word. The stars look completely random.

And then there's the stupid moon.

It's like it's making fun of me.

I throw it onto the floor in a huff.

Then I rip the stars all down and start over. This time going about the process in a more meticulous fashion, measuring it all out on paper before I place the stars to form each letter.

Hours later, my stomach growling and my arms aching from being up above my head for so long, I decide it's finished.

It's already dark, but I close my blinds anyway, turn off the lights, then collapse onto my bed.

It takes a few minutes for the stars to glow, but when they do, I can't help but smile.

She's going to love it.

I hope.

And after she says *yes*, I'm going to tell her that I know who she really is.

I fall asleep thinking how amazing it's going to be.

As I'm leaving the field house, I notice Keatyn slip behind the bushes not far from the door. I'm going to say something witty, but then I see Dawson get into a limo with Whitney.

Are they going to leave without her or did she decide not to go?

Wait, did she and Dawson break up?

I want to jump for joy and then kiss her, but her body language changes. Her shoulders slump forward in defeat, and I realize she's not happy about whatever just transpired.

"Why are we hiding in the bushes?" I whisper. "Aren't you going with them?"

As she turns around, her chest brushes across mine—the unmistakable jolt of energy I know we both feel every time we touch causing her to hop backwards and almost fall into the bushes. I reach out and grab her, holding her upright.

Tears fill her gorgeous eyes.

"Whitney told me right before the game was over that even though I was sitting there when she asked, that I wasn't invited. Then she said something nasty about me being Dawson's flavor of the week and how he's going to hook up with Rachel. I was going to cancel on him anyway. I have a car coming to pick me up in the morning and then I'm going to New York. I guess Dawson is still

44

mad at me about today. Or maybe Whitney is right, and I am just the flavor of the week."

I listen to her every word, thrilled that she's standing here in my arms, but mad that my sister and her friends could be so mean.

"You know, you're even beautiful when you cry," I say, brushing a few tears from her cheek.

"If this is the new and improved Aiden, I like him better already."

I realize I need to do what's best for her, not me. "I think you should still go. Show Whitney that she doesn't affect you. You have to stand up to bullies."

"I'm not sure I'm strong enough for that. Not with everything that happened today."

I give her a reassuring hug and whisper in her ear. "Everything will be okay, I promise."

She smiles through her tears. "You're right, Aiden. Thank you."

I take her hand and lead her to the limo.

The door opens. Whitney gets out, and Keatyn gets in.

I turn around and make my way back to the field house, wondering why I did that.

Whitney joins me. "I didn't think you'd be able to talk her into coming," she says with an evil laugh. "Which is ironic, because now she's going to get what she's got coming."

"What are you talking about?"

Whitney pulls out a gun and shoots me.

Bang. Bang.

I can feel each bullet slicing through my flesh. Burning.

Pain.

Whitney pulls off a mask, revealing that it's not really her but rather a man with dark hair and menacing eyes.

The man says, "Thank you for helping me set this all up."

This man must be the stalker.

And I led her straight to him.

I have to save her.

When I move to take a step forward, I collapse onto the ground.

I look up, seeing the man, shoving Keatyn back into the limo, a gun pointed at her head.

I know that I'm dying.

That the stalker has Keatyn because of me.

And there's nothing I can do to protect her.

Everything isn't *going to be alright.*

I wake up, white light blinding me. Thank goodness, it was just a dream.

But then I touch my chest, feel the bullet holes, and see my blood pumping out from my chest and pooling on the pristine floor underneath me.

Is this heaven? Am I dead?

My father's face appears before me. "I told you that you can't demand someone's trust. You have to earn it. And, now, look what you've done."

The blood on the floor turns into red hot flames, burning me alive.

As the fire sears my skin, I realize too late that I forced her trust rather than earned it. I screwed up again.

I want to fix it, but it's too late.

"Keatyn!" I cry out, the flames engulfing me as I look up and notice the glow-in-the dark stars above my head spelling out Homecoming?

I wake with a start, in a pool of sweat, her name still on my lips, light pouring in from the curtains I forgot to close last night.

I touch my chest, finding it intact, pain still fleeting across it.

It felt so real. Was it a premonition?

I grab my laptop and search. This one more important. I search a combination of *Abby Johnston* and *stalker*, then *Keatyn Douglas* and *stalker*, then *Abby Johnston's daughter* and *stalker*.

When nothing comes up, I do the same searches replacing *stalker* with *kidnapping*.

Nothing.

I lie back down and look up at the stars, barely distinguishable in the daylight, and think about her. My life was a mess when I made a wish on the moon. I'm tired of girls who only need a smile from me, a few shots, or a good game. I know the moon brought her to me. She is the kind of epic love I want.

I think about my parents. How when my mom got cancer, everything in my father's life stopped. How he sold the business he worked so hard to create. How he changed their lives completely. At the time, I thought he went a little overboard with it all. But I get it now.

He wanted the world for her, and he was going to give it to her, no matter how long they had left together.

I think about Brooklyn, the stalker, Dawson, my family.

And her.

When she kicked the soccer ball at my head, I knew.

As naturally as I knew the sound of my own heartbeat.

Knew we belonged together forever.

Now, I just need to prove it to her.

Even if I have to go a little overboard.

Monday, September 26th
CLAPPING AND SCREAMING.
LUNCH

I'M WAITING OUTSIDE the student center when I spot Keatyn for the first time today. She's talking with Jake and Bryce, and I'm trying to decide if I should interrupt them. But then I overhear them telling her they have to go do something for football, but to meet them at the lunch table.

She argues with them but eventually agrees.

She has on a pair of shoes I haven't seen before. Red suede platforms that have leopard print on the heel. She looks adorable and confident as she struts toward me.

But then she stops again, looking down at her phone.

She appears to type in a few replies, then the smile slides off her face, and she turns white, like she might faint. I wonder if it's more bad news from home. Something about the stalker.

She closes her eyes tightly to steady herself, then furiously texts. I stay where I am and wait for her.

After a few minutes, she puts her phone in her bag and walks toward me, but she seems caught up in thought. When I realize she hasn't even noticed me, I step directly in front of her.

"Are you okay?" I ask.

"Huh?" she says, distractedly. "Oh, yeah. I'm fine. My friend is safe. It's all good." But I know she's lying. She's upset about something else. She reaches out and touches my arm. "Hey, I heard you were the one who told Riley about what Whitney did. That was really nice."

"Well, I promised to be nice to you. Will you meet me in my room tonight for tutoring?"

"I appreciate it, Aiden. And, uh, sure."

We walk through the lunch line together but sit at different tables, her taking a spot next to my sister, who told me earlier today that Dawson didn't ask Keatyn to Homecoming this weekend.

I don't even feel jealous that she's going to sit with Dawson at lunch. In a few short hours, I'll be asking her to Homecoming.

I set my lunch tray down next to Parker and across from Logan.

Alicia and Ashley set their trays down on the table and take the two empty seats next to Logan.

Alicia runs her hand through Logan's hair and then kisses him.

I glance at Maggie, who frowns and looks away, even though Parker is holding her hand.

The Dean stands up in front of us and taps on a microphone. "I have a few announcements," he says.

As I swivel in his direction, Ashley taps my foot under the table, getting my attention. She gives me a sexy smirk then slides her bare foot up my leg then straight toward my crotch.

The Dean makes a few announcements that I'm not listening to, because I'm trying to get Ashley to get her damn foot off me without making a scene.

Just as I get her to comply, I hear the Dean say, "Keatyn Monroe, it's come to my attention that you've been seen canoodling around campus with Dawson Johnson."

Canoodling? What does that even mean?

I turn around in my seat to face the stage at the end of the cafe. Why would the Dean say something like that in public?

He continues. "I know you're new, but we have very high standards here."

Whitney laughs so loud that the whole lunchroom can hear. "This is priceless," she says, and my mind starts going crazy, wondering what Whitney has done now.

Did she tell the Dean something that will get Keatyn in trouble? Is she trying to get her kicked out of school?

I grab my phone and text my sister.

Me: *What has Whitney done?*
Peyton: *I have no idea.*
Me: *You have to stop it.*

The Dean continues. "You're about to see just how high."

Then the room fills with the sound of stripper music. The Dean drops the microphone and starts dancing.

And he doesn't dance very well. I should teach him a thing or two.

Everyone at our table is both laughing hysterically and cheering him on.

I glance at Peyton. She shakes her head at me. She has no idea.

The Dean sticks his index finger in his mouth then touches it to his ass. Like it's sizzling hot.

I can't help but laugh, too.

The side door opens. Jake, Riley, Bryce, Dallas, Tyrese, Ace, and some other guys on the team dance their way into the room.

This must be some skit.

The guys line up next to the Dean and do a striptease dance, pulling their school blazers off and tossing them to the ground.

All the girls at our table start clapping and screaming.

I look at Keatyn, see her shimmying to the music.

Whitney leans over and says something into Keatyn's ear, and I laugh as I watch Keatyn flip her the bird. Then she stands up, pumps her fist in the air, and screams.

All the guys except for Jake strip off their oxfords—the Dean included—and swing them above their heads like lassos.

This is crazy. And fun. My guess is this is something to boost ticket sales for the Homecoming game. But then why would the Dean have mentioned Keatyn's name?

Jake dances up to Keatyn and crooks his finger at her. She skips up to him as he pulls her into his hips and grinds against her.

You've got to love her spontaneity. From the look on her face, she has no clue what's going on either. They must have chosen her because they knew she'd love being on stage in front of everyone. That she'd dance and have fun. She's not afraid to make a fool of herself.

It's one of the many things I love about her.

Next thing I know, she's unbuttoning his shirt, dropping low and shaking her ass. Jake pulls her up and puts her arms in the air then slides his hands from the tips of her fingers down the sides of her chest to her waist.

I curl my fists into balls and swallow hard, immediately feeling jealous and wanting nothing more than to run up there and rip his hands clean off his body.

She runs her finger down the front of his shirt.

Jake pushes her back a little and says, "Get ready."

The music switches and the lyrics scream, *Aaaaare yooooou readyyyyy?* The crowd yells back, "YES!" Then a fast techno beat blares through the speakers.

The Dean jumps out from the line and rips his t-shirt straight down the middle. On his white pasty chest is a red painted **H**.

Jake follows suit. Ripping his shirt down the middle. On his chest is a red **O**.

What? No. No. No. No.

Riley jumps up in line and goes next. On his chest is the letter **M**. And on down the line, boys rip their shirts off, reveal their chests and a red letter. **E. C. O. M. I. N. G.**

Dawson is asking Keatyn to Homecoming. Before I get the chance.

This can't be happening.

Dawson slides in at the end of the line.

He hands her a bouquet of pink roses, then very slowly rips his shirt off too. On his chest there is a **?**

I watch in horror as he says, "What do you say, Keatie? Will you go to Homecoming with me?"

Please, say no. Please, say no.

But she screams out, "Yes," jumps into his arms, and gives him a steamy kiss.

I can't bear to watch, so I turn back around and stare at my lunch, feeling much like I did in my dream last night—like I was just shot in the chest and can't breathe.

"Wasn't that an amazing way for Dawson to ask Keatyn to

Homecoming, Aiden?" Ashley asks, rubbing it in.

No fucking way I'm asking her.

I get up, leaving my lunch, and march out of the cafe.

I SIT ON a bench, feeling defeated and wallowing in self-pity until I see students making their way to their afternoon classes.

I consider skipping French. How am I supposed to go sit behind her and smell her cotton-candy-scented hair every time she moves after this?

YOU HAVE A WILD SIDE.
FRENCH

KEATYN FLOATS HER way into class looking like she's on cloud nine.

I hate her.

"Well, that was something," I say flatly. I must be a glutton for punishment because I can't help wondering if she would have liked my proposal better.

She turns around and faces me. She's beaming. Obviously, she loved the way Dawson asked.

"Wasn't it outrageous? The way he asked. I loved it!"

"You like stuff like that? Being the center of attention." I roll my eyes toward the ceiling and laugh. I'm such an idiot. "Never mind. Don't answer that. Of course, you do. You seemed to be enjoying yourself. So, how come you never danced like that when we danced? It was pretty sexy."

"Oh gosh, did I look stupid?"

"No, everyone loved how you played along. You looked

shocked. Were you?"

"I had no clue. I thought I was in trouble. Even when the Dean started dancing, I thought it was some new girl hazing or something."

"You have a wild side." Something I hadn't considered.

"Everyone does. Do you?"

"You have a boyfriend now. You probably won't be finding out," I snap.

"If I was wild, that wouldn't stop me," she fires back.

I gaze at her for a beat. "No, I guess it wouldn't," I mutter out.

"You're right though," she says, practically bouncing in her seat. God, she looks beautiful. And happy. The bad part of all this is, I like seeing her happy. Even though I'm miserable. "I would never cheat, but he only asked me to Homecoming. Not to be his girlfriend."

Annie sits down and grabs Keatyn's arm. "That was so adorable! I can't believe you danced with Jake like that! Whitney was seething! It was awesome!"

"Just before it all started, Whitney was telling me that Dawson was going to ask her to Homecoming. Telling me how they bonded in the limo. How they will be King and Queen."

Annie sighs. "Don't do anything to make her mad at you, Keatyn. She's not a nice person."

She nods. One would expect that after what Whitney pulled this weekend, Keatyn would already know that.

She swivels in her seat, facing me again. "You know, it's because of you that Dawson and I are still together. I haven't thanked you properly, but what you did—how you told Riley. Seriously, thank you."

I close my eyes and swallow back my anger, grinding my pencil into my notebook instead of yelling at her for how dumb she is for being with Dawson. How she should be with me. But I can't. Especially now that I know what's she's going through. I lean closer to her and whisper, "I told you in the chapel that I'm done pretend punching your head."

She smiles. It kills me. "I'm glad, Aiden. I don't like when we fight."

I smile back. I can't help it. But at the same time, she's with him. He won. I lost. In fact, tonight at tutoring, I'm going to shove her lies in her face and threaten to tell her Homecoming date all about it. Screw it.

"I'm done fighting," I tell her.

She doesn't say anything in reply. Just slumps her shoulders, like what I said upset her, then turns around.

Wait. Does she want me to fight for her?

THIS IS FAMILIAR.
2:45PM

I'M AT FOOTBALL practice when I notice Keatyn running toward me, her long blonde hair flying behind her. She's changed out of her soccer clothes and into a skimpy dance outfit.

Damn.

"Hey, would it be okay if we did tutoring in your room tonight?" she asks, slightly out of breath. "Everyone is talking about lunch, about how Dawson asked me to Homecoming, and I know if we go to the library we won't get anything done because people will come up to gush about it."

"Uh," I say, trying to take my eyes off her long legs. "I'm sure the library will be fine."

She scrunches up her nose at me, probably because usually I'm trying to get her to come to my room so we can be alone.

But I can't have her come to my room tonight. I have to take down the damn stars first.

"Please," she says with a pout, moving closer to me—so close, I can see the purple glints.

"Oh, fine," I say, tilting my head and watching the shake of her skirt as she walks away.

"Seriously, Dawson is going to pummel you if you keep messing with her," Logan says, snapping me out of my reverie and making me mentally kick myself for agreeing. I swear, it's like her eyes have some power over me.

"It's just tutoring," I tell him.

"Yeah, sure it is. I heard what Ashley said at lunch. I'm sorry you had to watch Dawson ask Keatyn to Homecoming. I know what that feels like."

"Thanks. You're right. She's with Dawson. I need to back off," I lie.

I RUSH UP the stairs, knowing I'm late, to find her sitting against the wall in front of my dorm room, her eyes closed, in the exact spot she was the night of the party when I fixed her lips. I can't help but hope that's what she's thinking about right now.

I slide down the wall next to her. "Sorry, I'm late."

"It's okay," she says with a nod. "I haven't been waiting that long."

I can't help but smile at the two of us sitting here. In the exact same spot. "This is familiar."

"What is?" she says, pretending not to know exactly what I'm talking about.

"Don't you remember the party? When I kissed you right here?" I gently touch her lips with my finger. "Fixed your lips."

"Yeah, I remember, Aiden," she says with a sigh.

She starts to get up, but I grab her arm. "Why don't we just sit out here and study? Um, my room's a mess."

"You're such a liar," she says, calling me on it. "Your room is always perfect."

I roll my eyes, knowing I need to be firm about this. "I think out here would be better."

"Aiden, what is in your room?"

"I just . . . there's something I don't want you to see, okay?"

She squints her eyes at me, looking curious, then gets up and opens my door.

She looks around. Thank God, she doesn't look up. "It looks normal."

Maybe she won't even notice them. "Okay, well, let's get to it." I set my backpack on the ground and pull out my French workbook.

She does the same, taking it out and setting it on my desk.

"It's been an exhausting, crazy day," she says, flopping down on my bed.

Shit. Don't look up. Don't look up.

But part of me wants her to look up.

She looks around my room again then closes her eyes and says, "Okay, so I worked on the first page of our homework during drama today. Do you want to copy it and just go over it? It's mostly review."

"Uh, sure," I reply. "Give me a minute."

I grab her notebook and start copying.

"You don't have the twinkle lights on," she says. "It looks weird."

I glance up from my notebook and notice her looking at the ceiling. Spit catches in my throat, causing me to cough.

I changed my mind. I don't want her to see it.

But she does. Her eyes go wide and she says, "Aiden! Oh my gosh! You put up stars. Are they the glow-in-the-dark kind? I love those! My little sisters had them all over the ceilings of their bedrooms." She keeps studying them, apparently not realizing what it says yet. "Are they in a pattern?"

"Yeah, they're in a pattern." I tap my pencil on my workbook, getting agitated. "You were the one who wanted to come here so we wouldn't get distracted. Let's focus on French. We have a lot to do."

"No. I want to see them lit up first. I'm gonna turn your lights off for a minute."

I immediately move to the bed, blocking her from getting up.

I stare into her eyes, desperately trying to tell her that I love her. That she should be with me. That I spent eight hours yesterday working on this just for her.

"What?" she says.

"I didn't want you to see this, but I know you won't stop bugging me." Because she won't.

"That is true. Can I turn off the lights now?" She smirks at me. She loves getting her way almost as much as I love giving it to her.

"No. We're gonna do this my way. Scoot over to the edge of the bed and then close your eyes."

I know she hates being told what to do, but for once, she

complies.

"You promise to keep them closed until I tell you to open them?" I ask. If I'm going to do this, I'm going to do it right.

"Sure."

"Okay." I flip off the light. Then I pull down my blinds and close my blackout drapes.

I look at her, lying perfectly still on my bed, her hair splayed out around her face. The curves of her body rising and falling in all the right places. God, she's beautiful.

I lie down next to her, allowing our shoulders to touch, then reach my pinkie out and take ahold of hers like it's the most natural thing in the world—and it feels like it is. "Open your eyes now."

I turn to face her, watching the emotions cross her face. First, she seems to just take all the stars in, then she squints slightly, and I can tell she's realized what it spells out. She smiles broadly, but then the smile fades, and she frowns.

Her breathing speeds up, and she moves her hand to her stomach, clutching it.

Not what I was expecting.

Just as I'm about to tell her the truth, she leaps off the bed, grabs her workbook and backpack, and bounds toward my door.

But she gets tangled up with my chair.

She and the chair do a sort of slow-motion dance before it darts out from underneath her and sends her crashing to the ground.

I jump off the bed to help her, but she gets up and says, "I'm fine. I'm not feeling well all of a sudden. I'm sorry. I, uh, I have to go. Call Annie if you need help."

Then she rushes out of the door, slamming it behind her.

I turn on the lights, extinguishing the stars, then call Logan to see if he wants to go off campus for dinner. I can't bear facing her again tonight. This was bad enough.

UNFORTUNATELY FOR ME, he invites Alicia who invites Ashley, who won't stop talking about Homecoming. I consider taking her to my room after dinner, showing her the damn stars, and asking her.

There's really no reason why I shouldn't.

Logan invites the girls to come to our dorm before curfew. Ashley reaches out and takes my hand. I allow it this time, figuring what the heck. I'll ask her.

We run into Riley in the hallway. He's carrying what appears to be a bloody sock.

"What the hell is that?" Logan asks, the girls agreeing with a screech.

"Keatyn fell and cut her knee. It was bleeding really bad. She had to get five stitches."

I drop Ashley's hand, immediately feeling sick to my stomach. Did she cut her knee when she fell on my chair? Was she so upset that she didn't notice how bad it was?

Why did the stars upset her so much? Is it because she wishes she would have said no to Dawson and yes to me? Or did she think they were for someone else?

"Um, I'm not feeling so well," I say to everyone, rushing off to my room.

When I open my door, the stars are glowing.

I consider grabbing the ladder and ripping them all down. But I can't.

For some damn reason, I just can't.

Tuesday, September 27th

FIVE STITCHES.

7AM

I HIGHLY DOUBT Keatyn will be at our Social Committee meeting this morning. I consider going back to sleep, hating how early our meetings are.

But I go anyway, on the off chance that I'll get to see her. Sit with her. Spend time with her.

When I arrive, I see her sitting in a chair, pulling her sock down, and inspecting the gauze over her cut.

I sit down next to her. "Five stitches, huh?"

"Yeah," she slurs.

"Why did you run out of my room and pretend you weren't hurt, when you obviously were?"

"I felt sick. I didn't really know about the cut until I saw it was bleeding."

Peyton and Brad start the meeting, so I stop talking.

Peyton goes through all the details for the Homecoming after party. I watch Keatyn struggling to stay awake.

They must have given her some pain medication.

I let her sleep for a bit, but then wake her toward the end of the meeting.

"Boots," I whisper. "I think you dozed off."

"Oh, I'm sorry," she says, as Brad goes over more details.

Considering she's a little messed up, I figure I might as well make one last effort. "Will you save me a dance at the after party?"

"I don't know," she says with a playful smirk. "Can you dance?"

Can I dance? Of course, I can dance.

But . . . an idea pops into my brain.

I put my head down in embarrassment.

It works. She says, "Oh my gosh. Is that why you only wanted to dance to slow songs? Is that all you know how to do?"

"I'll get my French homework done before tutoring. You can teach me to dance instead."

"I don't really feel like dancing, Aiden. The knee and all."

No way she's getting off that easily.

"I've gone above and beyond the call of duty in Social Committee. It's not something I really had the time to do, but I did it for you. So you owe me."

NO RHYTHM.
4:40PM

KEATYN IS IN my room after school, getting ready to teach me how to dance.

"This is silly," she says. "I can't teach you how to dance. Plus, I'm injured."

"I saw you jogging at soccer practice, even though I doubt

62

you were supposed to."

She giggles. "I took another pain pill. Felt healed."

I raise an eyebrow at her, causing her to give me a dramatic sigh. She turns on a dance playlist, grabs my hips, and moves them to the beat.

Well, tries to.

I pretend to have no rhythm.

She seems to give up, turning around. I'm about to tell her the truth when she stands in front of me, pushes her back firmly into my chest, and pulls my arm around her waist.

Then she grinds her ass into me.

Holy shit.

I grind back, forgetting that I'm not supposed to know how and simply loving the feel of her body—and kinda wishing we were naked. I consider sliding my hands up her skirt.

She puts her hands on top of mine and moves them around her body in the name of dancing.

And I'm pretty sure I've died and gone to heaven.

AFTER ABOUT SIX songs, there's a moment when I feel myself start to harden. I've been controlling myself pretty well up until now, but she just slid my hand across from her stomach down further. And there's only so much a guy can take.

So I don't embarrass myself, I spin her out of my arms and break out my dance moves.

"What the hell?" she says with a genuine look of surprise on her face. "Did you used to be in a boy band? Are you here in some embarrassment protection program?" I give her a sneaky grin as she shakes her head at me. "Don't tell me you can sing, too."

Now that I've regained control, I find myself going back for more. "We'll have to save that for another day, Boots. I don't want to overwhelm you with all my talents at once."

"Everyone says you have great hands," she says.

"These?" I ask, holding them up in front of her.

She studies them, then glides a finger across my pinkie and middle finger. "What happened here?"

"Knife attack. In the war," I tease.

"Very funny."

"Fine. Cleat attack."

"Now I know why you're such a good goalie," she says, further examining my hands.

"Because I'm fast." I quickly slap the tops of her hands. Like the game we used to play when we were kids.

She slaps mine back quickly, surprising me. "Not fast enough," she says with an adorable smirk. She takes my hands in hers again, holding them up and scrutinizing them. "They're too big for your body."

"What do you mean?"

"Proportionately. They're off. They're too big." She tilts her head at me, taking in my six-foot-two-inch frame. "That, or you're not done growing yet."

"I'm probably not done growing yet," I shrug, then start doing the robot to the music. I'd much rather be dancing with her.

"You *so* know how to dance," she says with a laugh.

"Naw, you're just a really good teacher. I couldn't do this until today."

"You're such a liar. How do you know how to dance like this? You dance alone in your room to music videos or something?"

"No. I have a bossy older sister."

"So?"

"So, instead of wanting to play school or Barbies, she wanted to play dance instructor. If I played nice, she snuck me cookies."

"So everyone at school knows you can dance like this but me, right? Very funny. Ha. Ha. You tricked me."

I take a step closer to her, wrap my arm around her waist, and put my leg between hers—our lower halves entwining in an intimate way.

"You're the only one at school who knows I can dance like this. Well, besides my sister."

"Why?"

"Because it's embarrassing. You asked me if I was in a boy band witness protection program or something."

"Ohmigawd, did your mom video tape it? I'm so asking your sister."

I stifle a laugh. Seriously, she's so cute. And I have so much fun with her. Doing nothing. Although with the heat radiating off her leg, I probably can't call this nothing. Somehow, I don't think Dawson would be thrilled to see us like this. Not that I care. I practically live for these moments. And tonight has just reconfirmed what my heart says—she's not in love with Dawson. And that means I still have a chance. "You are not. Or you'll be in trouble."

"Oh, really?" she sasses, getting in my face. "What kind of trouble?"

I grab her ass firmly in each hand, squeeze it, and raise an eyebrow in challenge.

She does the same, grabbing the back of my jeans. She licks her lips as she pulls my shirt up over my head and tosses it on the floor.

I slide my hands across her curves, from her thin waist to her slender hips.

She responds by gliding her fingers down my sides.

"You gonna do that at the dance?" I ask.

"Maybe." She plants her palms firmly on my pecs, then closes her eyes and dances with me—grinding on my leg.

I don't care anymore if she can tell how much she turns me on.

When we danced during our twenty-nine songs, it was our bodies pressed together and swaying, barely moving and completely caught up in each other. This is different—a playful mix of crazy fun and sinfully sexy foreplay.

A FASTER SONG starts, and she pushes off my chest, jumps up and down, then turns around and shakes her shapely ass at me. It takes everything I have not to pick her up, throw her on my bed, and ravish her.

But I'm enjoying this moment with her too much. There will be plenty of time for that later, so I spin her around and put my knee back between her legs.

She runs her hands over my shoulders, so I start a fast, exaggerated version of a waltz—pulling her toward me, spinning her out, then back in tightly to my chest.

She's only wearing a little bra top, so I place my hand on her bare stomach and caress it, causing her to reach up and wrap her arm around my neck.

I drop my head, allowing our cheeks to touch. Even though the beat is fast, our bodies have slowed down. I let my hands roam slowly across her body, causing her to shiver in their wake.

Then the music stops.

She turns around to face me.

Our faces are so close.

Our lips torturously closer.

My hand tangles in her hair, and I look into her eyes, knowing they convey both fire and love.

She lets out a big breath of air, her posture suddenly shifting.

"I think you're ready for the dance," she says, grabbing her jacket from my chair.

I steal it from her and plop down on the futon.

"Dance for me," I command. I'm not ready for her to leave, and I could tell by the look on her face, she just thought about Dawson. About how she shouldn't have been dancing with me like that. But she couldn't really help it. She belongs with me.

"Dance for you?" she asks.

"Yeah."

"You wanna see my Kiki stripper moves?" she laughs, trying to make a joke. "Cuz I really don't have any."

"No. I want to see you move. Show me your new routine. My sister's been telling me about it."

"I can't show you. It's totally top secret."

"It's either that or I pull you on this futon and make a cheater out of you." And I'm so not kidding at this moment. Her hands all over me have left me on fire.

"Look, Aiden. It's nice that we're getting along better. But I like Dawson, and I shouldn't have danced with you like that. I don't want to give you the wrong idea. So if I'm going to keep tutoring you, it'll have to be in the library. No more dances. No more almost kisses. No more talking on my neck."

"But you and Dawson aren't exclusive. You still aren't wearing the key. So go on a date with me. Date us both."

She seems to consider this by staring into my eyes, maybe trying to decide if I'm serious or not.

"I'm sorry, Aiden, but I can't date a guy like you. A guy who can't decide if he loves me or hates me." I'm going to counter her argument, tell her how I feel, but she says, "And I know we had some crazy love at first sight thing, but we obviously would be a disaster together."

She felt it, too.

I can't help but grin. She just admitted that she loves me.

A smile spreads across my face. I tap my foot, my whole body practically humming.

"Why are you grinning?"

"Love at first sight, huh?"

"No. It's just an expression. That stuff doesn't happen in real life," she says, unconvincingly.

I stand up and move close, my chest touching hers. She sucks in a breath and moves slightly backward.

But when she takes a step back, I take another step forward.

She takes another step backward into my wall. Now there's nowhere for her to go.

I put my palms on the wall, boxing her in. The fire I've been feeling—the desire—is practically radiating off my body. I've never felt this kind of hunger before.

She sighs and closes her eyes.

I let my cheek graze against hers as I whisper in her ear. If she wants to play hard to get, well, two can play at that game. "I think being just your friend will be fun."

She doesn't open her eyes, just pants out, "How so?"

Dancing like we just did comes to mind, but that was more

than friendly. I open my mouth, place it on her cheek, then slowly pucker, forming a kiss. Then I gently pull my top lip off her cheek first, the bottom lip staying in place and then—bit by agonizing bit—receding.

Her eyes fly open in shock.

"I have to go."

"See ya, friend," I say playfully, but I don't move. Just raise one of my hands off the wall, giving her a small pathway to squeeze through.

Then she's out the door.

But it doesn't matter, because I know how she really feels. I just need her to stop fighting it.

As I'm lying in my bed later that evening, I realize that it might be more. I try to put myself in her shoes. What if I had to leave home? What if even though I was making friends with everyone here, I knew I was lying to them. She said she hates having to lie to people. It's got to be hard for her. Tonight, although amazing, ended with her leaving pissed off.

She's probably not going to trust—let alone, let herself love—someone who does nothing but piss her off.

I need to be her friend first, I think, if I want to become her everything.

Wednesday, September 28th
STOP GRINNING.
FRENCH

BACK IN FRENCH and Keatyn hasn't spoken to me at all day. So I'm surprised when she spins around and says to me, "Isn't Logan one of your best friends?"

"Yeah. Why?"

"I heard he's trying out for the part of the Bad Prince."

I can't help but frown as I nod yes. Logan really wants the part. Probably because he will act like a playboy in it. And he'll be kissing numerous girls on stage.

"Is he nice?"

"Logan?" I ask.

"Yeah. He's in my math class. Sits right in front of me. He has a nice looking back, but that's all I know about him. I tried to talk to him yesterday about the play. I don't think he likes me." She sighs. "And I'm not sure why."

"Uh, that's probably my fault," I reply, knowing full well why he doesn't like her.

"Your fault?"

I push my pencil around in a tight circular motion before

raising my head. I don't want to answer this question. But, if I want her to be honest with me, I suppose I need to be honest in return. "I may have told him about some of my past frustrations with you."

"So he hates me," she says flatly, putting her head down and turning back around.

Once again, she's mad at me.

Annie looks over at her. "What's wrong? You look like you're going to cry."

I can tell by her motion that she wipes tears away, but she replies, "I think I have something in my eye."

I lean up and whisper in her ear. "He doesn't hate you."

She quickly turns back around, anger written all over her face.

"You must have had wonderful things to say about me to make him hate me when he doesn't even know me."

"He thinks you kind of played me."

"Played you? Are you kidding me? You're the one who got all pissed off and didn't call."

"He's also sort of down on love."

"That must be why he wants to play the Bad Prince. He'll get to be the cynic."

I nod, agreeing. "He is kind of cynical about love."

She gazes into my eyes and, I swear, all I see reflected there is love—no trace of anger, just maybe a little bit of hurt. She sits up straighter and changes the subject. "I think it's funny that Jake is trying out for the part of the Good Prince. He's so not good."

"He's a Prefect," I counter.

She grins. "Yeah, but he's naughty." *I can be naughty too, Keatyn,* I think. "I love that about him."

Love. "You said that so easily."

"Said what?"

"That you love him."

"Well, not *in* love. That's different." It sure is.

"Have you told Dawson you love him yet?"

She fidgets nervously. "I told him that I'm ready for the key."

"That's not what I asked." Is it bad that I want to shout for joy? That I'm thrilled she isn't ready to say she loves him, because it just might mean that she's in love with me.

"Well, that's all I'm answering because it's none of your business what I say to him."

I can't help but smile. Big.

"Stop grinning," she says, swiveling back around in her seat. "It's annoying."

And awesome.

FEEL LIKE GIVING UP.
LATE

I'M IN MY room studying when my sister calls me.

"Hey, what's up?"

"Just studying."

"Can we party in your room tonight?"

"I'm tired, Peyton. I don't really feel like partying. I just want to go to bed."

"Aiden, I really need to blow off some steam. Please," she begs. "You can go sleep in Bryce's room if you don't feel like partying. You do that all the time."

"Why should I?"

"Because you love your sister?"

I look up at the stars on the ceiling. No one has seen them, and I want to keep it that way.

"Who's all coming?"

"You know, the usual. Dawson, Keatyn, Jake, Whitney, Bryce, and whoever else I feel like hanging out with."

I glance at the clock. It's already past curfew. That doesn't give me much time.

"Sure," I say, giving in.

I put my homework down and set up the ladder. With each star I pull from the ceiling, I think about all the memories I've had with Keatyn this year in my room already.

Maybe I should tell her they were for her.

Only for her.

I'm tempted to throw them away, but I just can't. It's like admitting defeat so, instead, I pack them all away in a shoebox.

I'm putting them in the closet when my sister barges into my room.

"I thought you were tired?" she says. "Change your mind? Let's do a shot before everyone gets here."

"Naw. I'm still not finished with my homework." I pick up my notebook and head toward the door. "Have fun tonight."

She gives me a hug as I'm leaving. "You're seriously the best brother ever."

I GO ACROSS the hall to Bryce's room, feeling depressed. You'd think looking at the stars every night would be what would depress me, but for some strange reason they sort of gave me hope.

"You're not partying with us?" Bryce asks, upon seeing my arms full of books.

"Too much homework," I lie, but really, I don't want to see Keatyn and Dawson all lovey dovey. It's one thing to have to endure it at school, but another thing entirely in my room.

He grabs a bottle of rum and heads out the door. "Come over after you're finished."

I'm trying to concentrate on my French assignment, but I can hear their voices.

Hear Keatyn's laughter.

Sometimes I feel like giving up.

I tear a page out of my notebook and write on it.

Why should I bother?

I lie here and think about it while doodling on the page. Why should I?

I can't come up with a good answer, so I write down my vocabulary words, making sure I know how to spell each one. Then I go back to doodling.

I hear her laughter again, the melody like a song that plays over and over in my head. If I could hear her laugh every day of my life, I would die a happy man.

Then I remember what she said the other day. About how we were love at first sight. Until that moment, I didn't know if she felt it too.

I look up the translation for my answer in French and add it to the paper.

Elle ressentait la même chose.

She felt the same way. That's why I couldn't throw the stars away. That's why I can't lose hope.

I close my eyes for a moment and remember.

A FEW HOURS later, I wake up in total darkness with the covers pulled up around my shoulders. I click on the lamp. My French notebook, which was on my lap when I fell asleep, is on Bryce's desk.

I notice the pencil holder is tipped over and all the pencils on the desk. I get up and look at the alcohol stash and notice that the cake vodka I started buying just because she loves it is gone.

But then I panic, remembering what I had written before I went to sleep. I grab the workbook and find it shoved between the pages. Thank goodness.

I smile, imagining her turning off the light and covering me up.

Which is really kinda sweet.

Thursday, September 29th
WHO WAS THAT?
6PM

"YOU SHOULD COME watch us try out," Logan tells me as we're finishing up an early dinner.

"For the play?"

"Yeah," he says.

Alicia, who even though Logan has told her he's going stag to Homecoming hasn't stopped sitting with us, says, "I'll come watch you, Logan. And then I'll be cheering for you at the JV game tonight."

"That's great," he says without even a smile. I can tell he's already sick of her clinginess.

We all head to the theater, and I watch both he and Nick try out. I'm going to leave with him until I see the list of names and times each person is set to tryout. Keatyn is coming up soon. At seven.

"Hey, I'll see you later," I tell Logan as he leaves. He's running late and doesn't argue.

A short time later, someone calls out, "Keatyn Monroe."

Keatyn walks up onto the stage dressed in a swingy floral

print skirt, a lace top, and cowboy boots. She looks like the sweet Texas girl she's supposed to play.

While others haven't completely memorized their lines, she doesn't have a note in sight.

I say a little prayer that she will do a good job.

But from the second she says her first line, it's clear that she's better than good. Everyone who has been watching auditions knows it. They stop whispering and watch, drawn in by the ease of which she has become the Cheerleader Bachelorette.

Her voice even sounds different as she speaks in an authentic sounding Texas accent. It's like she's become a different person. Her demeanor, even her face, is softer. I almost start laughing when she puts her hand on her hip. When she does that, it usually means she's mad at me.

But on stage, it shows the character's sassy side.

It's amazing, really.

When she comes off the stage, she's beaming. It's easy to see it's where she belongs. Which considering who her mom is, it shouldn't surprise me, but it does. She's amazing.

She stops and types on her phone and then works her way to the back of the darkened auditorium where I'm sitting.

"Are you trying out?" she whispers as she takes a seat next to me.

"No, I watched Logan and Nick try out earlier. They had to get to the JV game. I decided to stay and watch for a while."

"Shouldn't you be there, too?"

"Cole was the starting receiver, and he got hurt, so I'm filling in for him and will only be playing Varsity for a while."

"That's exciting. Congrats."

I cock my head and study her. "So just *who* was that up

there?"

"What do you mean?" she asks, frowning. "Oh my gosh, did I suck?"

I smile at her and shake my head. "No, you didn't suck. It was like watching a different person. The accent. The way you flipped your hair. And you put your hand on your hip when she was being sassy. You only do that in real life when you're mad. You even held your jaw differently. Like, not as tight as usual and your face looked softer. Sweeter, maybe."

She gives me a dazzling smile. One that lights up the darkened corner we're in. "That's because she's not a bitch like I am."

"You're not a bitch."

"No? But I can play one." She straightens her back, tilts her chin, and looks down upon me. Then she rolls her shoulders forward and looks at me defiantly.

"Damn, you haven't even said anything yet, and I'm already scared," I tease. I study her face. "You know, you have a very expressive face."

"Thank you," she says.

"You belong up there. On stage. You made it look completely effortless, like you're a natural." Now would be the perfect time for her to tell me about her actress mom and her model dad.

But she doesn't.

Why doesn't she?

Instead, she nods her head and whispers so softly, I'm not even sure if she means for me to hear it. "I think it's what I want to do. Like, for a living. Like, if I'm good enough."

I want to pull her into my arms and tell her I know the truth. I want to tell her that I know it's probably hard to follow in her mother's footsteps. Because that would be a lot of pressure, now that I think about it.

"If I didn't need you here to tutor me, I'd suggest you quit school, go to Hollywood, and start auditioning. I'm serious, Keatyn."

"Um, uh, thanks," she stammers, getting unusually tongue-tied. "But I think I need some practice first. Some classes, maybe."

"Well, I know you'll get the part."

"You can't know that. I was the first one to audition for it."

"Why did you pick that role and not the lead?"

"I like how she affects the story, I guess. I like how she has to follow her heart and how she finds true love. How even though the Bad Prince tries to keep her and the Good Prince apart, their love prevails."

I let out a deep growl, some primal urge overcoming me. I want to be her Good Prince.

"I always knew you were a romantic at heart," I say, trying to cover it up.

She changes the subject.

"I've heard it's hard to be an actress. Dealing with the paparazzi. The filming locations. Kissing your cast mates. I can see why Dawson is having a hard time with it."

He's having a hard time with it? Awesome.

I lean closer to her and rest my hand on her knee. "Dawson should be here supporting you. And if he had come, he'd know. It's not you up there." Electric shivers shoot from her leg up my hand, making it hard for me to think straight. "You know, I'd love to watch you walk the red carpet someday."

Her pupils are wide, and she's looking a little crazed.

But then again, my hand is on her knee, and I'm feeling a

little crazed myself. There's no denying our chemistry.

"You'll walk the red carpet with me?" she asks, looking confused now.

I smile broadly. "I said I'd *watch* you walk it, but if you're offering . . ."

"Oh. I, um, just, you know, a hot guy in a black suit is, um, well, it's like the ultimate accessory."

I can't help but grin. "It's agreed then. I'll be your arm candy."

I lean back in my seat and watch the next audition, allowing what I told her time to sink in. When she grabs the key necklace that she's now wearing and slides it back and forth across her chin, I know that she's thinking about me. Or trying not to think about me.

We watch the rest of the auditions in silence.

Friday, September 30th
SOMETHING TO KEEP.
FRENCH

MY DAYS SEEM to revolve around waiting for French class. And especially today.

She slides into her desk just before the tardy bell rings.

"Congrats on the play. I told you you'd get the part."

She flips around. "What do you mean?"

"Didn't you hear the cast announcement at lunch?"

"No! I skipped lunch. I was helping your sister with some Social Committee stuff. Well, sorta."

"You're playing the part of the Cheerleader Bachelorette."

She lets out a loud shrill. "Ahhhh!"

Miss Praline goes, "Keatyn?"

She flips toward the front of the class. "I can't help it. I'm so excited!"

I explain, "She just found out she got the role she wanted in the school play."

"Well, that's nice, Miss Monroe," Miss Praline says. "Congratulations."

"I'm excited for you, Keatyn," Annie says. "But I'm even

more excited for tomorrow."

She grabs Annie's arm. "Oh, I didn't tell you about tonight, did I? Riley is going to ask Ariela right before the game. We're writing *Homecoming?* on a football, and he's going to pass it to her during warm-ups."

"Oh, that's so cute!" Annie gushes.

"And she'll be able to keep the football. I kind of wish I had something to keep."

"Me too," Annie says. "Although I do have a screen shot of him asking me. And Maggie took pictures."

I still have the stupid stars, I think.

She spins around. "What ever happened with your stars, Aiden? I keep thinking I'll see someone post them on Facebook."

"What stars?" Annie asks.

I ignore Annie and say in a stern voice, "I don't want to talk about it."

She looks hurt and turns back around.

I rake my fingers through my hair in frustration then lean down and pretend to be interested in doodling.

I pretend not to notice when she sneaks a peek back at me.

A few minutes later, she drops a note over her shoulder.

Why don't you want to talk about it?

Maybe I'm embarrassed about it.

Awwww. Aiden . . . Did she say no?

Not exactly. It just didn't work out.

I'm sorry.

And maybe I'm a glutton for punishment, but I have to ask.

What would you have said?

Like if I didn't have a boyfriend or a date already?

Yes, hypothetically. If someone asked you like that, would you have liked it?

If you would have laid next to her on the bed, touched her pinkie, and asked, I think it would have been perfect.

Better than naked chests?

Different than naked chests. The stars were romantic and they must have taken freaking FOREVER to hang up.

They were a pain in the ass. Kinda like the girl.

I probably shouldn't tell you this but shark told me in detention that you have a crush on someone who doesn't like you back. He said you've been waiting on the dream girl. I'm sorry it's not working out the way you want it to. It sucks to have a crush on someone and not have them like you back.

Note to self: Kill Shark.
But then I reread her comment.

You know how that feels? That surprises me.

Yes, I know how it feels. I crushed on someone for almost two whole years before anything happened between us. Why does that surprise you?

Was it the Keats guy?

Yeah. We were friends before we dated. So, don't give up on her. You know, like if you're not too mad about the stars and stuff. My step dad says sometimes true love takes a bit. So if she really is your dream girl, you shouldn't give up. But I thought the Keats guy was my dream guy.

He isn't.

Or at least he isn't right now. He loved me, but not . . . If that even makes sense.

Don't give up on her? Is she so completely clueless that she doesn't know I'm talking about her? Who does she think my dream girl is? I haven't been with anyone but her all semester.

What didn't he love about you? You seem fairly lovable.
I mean, when you're not annoying.

We're getting off topic here. I'm supposed to be helping you with your dream girl problems.

And I told you that I don't want to talk about it.
So stop asking.

You could tell me who she is. Then maybe I could help.

I don't think that would help. But maybe if I knew what happened with you and the Keats guy, I could avoid making the same mistakes with her.

I hate to break it to you, but if you asked her out and she said no, she maybe shouldn't be your dream girl.

Like, sometimes you think they are the dream.

But then they get mad at you for buying Italian leather in Italy.

But how could they? I mean, it's ITALY!!!!

And then they get mad at you for dancing on top of a bar or with guys at a club.

But sometimes you can't help yourself!

Cuz you like to have fun!

And sometimes when they don't want to have fun with you, they sit around and pout. That should probably tell you that it isn't going to work.

Unless they change.

But if you have to change for someone, then you are not still you, and that's bad too. You have to be careful not to lose yourself in the process.

I think . . .

Really, I'm rambling and I shouldn't have offered to help. I don't think I know what true love is. Or how to spot it. Every time I think I know, I'm proven wrong. Maybe that's what happened to you.

You were just wrong about it.

Love is a tricky bitch.

Do you know about the Greek goddess, Aphrodite?

I can't help but chuckle at her answer. I'm going to assume that's why she and Brooklyn are not together. He didn't appreciate her love of the spotlight.

She's the goddess of love, right?

Or, maybe, seduction. I think she's tricky, mostly. She teases us with the idea of love. She and Disney probably have a deal. Get young girls to watch princess movies. Get them to believe in fairytale endings. Then when they grow up, they will have unrealistic expectations of what true love is about.

I mean, seriously, do I think some guy is going to ride up on a white horse and rescue me and we'll fall in love and have little hottie babies and it will be all magical and amazing?

Actually, yes, I do.

It worked. That is what I want. That's really what EVERY girl wants.

But then there's Aphrodite. She gets you to fall in love.

Tricks you with sex and seduction. Then she names your baby AWFUL.

Or she makes you believe in soul mates. But then she sleeps with someone else. She lets guys quote you poetry, which makes you all swoon, but then you find out that they don't really mean it. They just want to sleep with you.

And then they're good in bed. And sweet. But you know the other shoe is gonna drop. So you are afraid to say it. To tell someone that you love them.

But then you do.

Because you believe in love.

Cuz, hell, I don't even know why. Because you just do. I mean who doesn't want to believe that their soul mate is out there? Their other half? The person who will love every annoying thing about them.

But, really, it's probably mostly bullshit.

That part about quoting her poetry. Does she think that I just wanted to sleep with her?

Just for the record, your lips were my bliss.

See. Case in point why love sucks. You were playing me. Telling me sweet stuff when you were really in love with someone else. You're lucky I'm even willing to try to be friends. I should hate you.

Actually, sometimes, I kinda do.

I grin.

Sometimes, I kinda hate you, too.

And that is what might save our friendship. We don't have to worry about having love get in the way. You love someone else (even though you probably shouldn't) and I'm in love with someone else.

(Even though you probably shouldn't.)
By the way, you haven't tutored me all week.

I know. I'm not sure I can tonight either.

I lean up and whisper in her ear. "You better be there, or I'll quit Social Committee."

"So quit. I'm tired of you telling me that. If you don't want to be there, then just quit."

I lean up a little closer and sigh. "I need you. Please?"

She turns around to answer me, but when she does, her cheek smashes into my lips.

"You want me to kiss you, all you have to do is ask. You don't have to try and be all sneaky about it."

She gets mad, whipping her head forward and flipping her hair in my face. "Kissing you is the *last* thing I want to do," she mutters.

"In your life?" I can't help but tease her. Even though I'm serious.

"What?"

"Are you telling me that will be your dying wish? *It's the last thing I want to do. Have his lips on mine. Then I can die happy,*" I say dramatically.

"You really should've tried out for the play. Drama king."

"I'm not a drama king."

"Ha! Everything about you is drama." She turns back around and smirks at me. "Big production. But no one is buying the tickets."

"And you're the little production that gets out of hand. Turns into a massive time and money pit. Then goes straight to DVD."

She looks hurt and tears spring into her eyes. "That's harsh." She dabs the corner of her eye for effect. Hangs her head down a little.

It's funny, but I can play along. I pretend to feel bad. "I was just teasing. I already told you that you'd get amazing reviews and I . . ."

She lets her face break into a wide shit-eating grin.

"Seriously? You can bring on the fake tears that easily?"

She shrugs a shoulder. "It's a gift."

YOU'RE NOT DEAD.
5:30PM

MY SISTER AND I are walking down to the field house together.

"Are you going to ask anyone to Homecoming?" she asks me. "Usually, you'd have a date by now."

"I think Logan and I are going stag," I reply noncommittally. "What about you?"

"I'm thinking of asking someone who doesn't go to the school. Maybe an alum."

"Just tell me it's not Camden."

She smirks. "Maybe."

"Why? After the shit he put you through. I don't even know how you could be friends with him after that."

"It's been a long time since Cam and I broke up. We've grown up. And there's no one here I want to date. They're all boys. I'm ready for a man."

I shake my head. "Sometimes I don't get you."

"I'm a woman. We change our minds. Get used to it."

As we enter the field house, I see Keatyn and Dawson standing by the locker room door, kissing.

Then he smacks her ass.

It takes everything I have not to go pound him into the ground.

Not to mention the fact that I'm pissed at Keatyn. She stood me up for tutoring today. Now I know why.

My sister gives her a smile as Keatyn heads in our direction.

I raise my eyebrows at her and frown. "So you're not dead."

Peyton smacks me on the shoulder. "Be nice."

"She ditched me."

"I did ditch him," Keatyn says. "I'm sorry. I, um . . . I had something else I needed to do, and I kinda forgot to text you."

Peyton giggles. "Was that thing you *needed to do* Dawson?"

Keatyn's mouth drops open. "Um . . ."

I shake my head at her.

"He's going home with his parents after the game, so I won't get to see him tonight. I just, we just, I wanted to say goodbye. And he . . ."

He's going away? A smile plays on my lips. "That's understandable," I say. "So then we'll have to do it tonight."

"You have a game."

"After the game. After curfew."

"Everyone is going to the Cave tonight."

"Everyone but us," I tell her. "We'll be in my room studying." Or dancing, hopefully.

"No. No, we won't."

"Will Dawson get jealous?"

"No, he has nothing to be jealous of, but I don't want anyone to get the wrong idea. I love Dawson."

I tilt my head at her. She told him she loves him?

"Yes, Aiden. I told Dawson I love him. Yes, I was confused for a while about love. That happens after you go through a break-up. It's normal to question it and become more cynical of love because you don't want to get hurt again. But Dawson's not going to hurt me."

"Awww," Peyton says. Quite honestly, I forgot my sister was still standing here. "When did you tell him?"

"It was the other night. I told him I hearted him. He asked if that was close to loving him. I hadn't said it because I was scared to. But he makes me happy, and I wanted him to know it."

"I love that feeling," Peyton gushes back. "It's so dream—"

I interrupt her. I don't need to hear this shit. "I'll let you ladies finish your love fest here. I have to get in the locker room." But before I leave, I gaze into Keatyn's eyes and say, "I know where we can go. I'll be outside your window at one. We'll study then go party with everyone."

"Really?" she asks.

I shrug. I can't have her thinking I'm going to sit around and wait for her. "What? You think you're the only one with plans?"

WHERE'S THE HAREM?
1AM

WHEN IT'S FINALLY time, I go to her room. Not that I've been counting down the minutes. Okay, maybe I have.

I knock on her window softly to let her know I'm here.

She slides out of it. I catch her. She looks so damn sexy. Her hair is down and curled. She's wearing jean shorts, a thermal shirt, and the boots she wore the day we met.

"What are you doing?" she says.

"Just catching you," I reply sweetly.

She tries to push out of my arms, but I hold firm. "You can let go now," she says.

I gently drop her to the ground and look at her feet. "You're wearing boots."

"I wear boots all the time."

"Not *those* boots. You haven't worn those since the day we met."

She rolls her eyes. "I've been sort of mad at them."

I tilt my head to the side and squint at her. "Mad at your boots? You can't be mad at *those* boots."

"I'm not anymore. We made up."

"Well, that's good to hear. Let's get French done so we can go party." I place my hand on the small of her back to guide her, causing her to jump.

"You're awfully jumpy tonight."

"Stop touching me then," she states a little too emphatically.

I do as she asks for the moment and lead her up to the chapel, which is open all night. Plus, it's sort of our place.

I know she probably thinks that since Dawson is gone I'm going to try to monopolize her time, but I'm not.

I study with her in an almost business-like fashion, working mostly on my word enunciation for the verbal portion of our upcoming test.

My phone keeps vibrating throughout our studying. I may have purposely texted a lot of people, knowing they would text me back while we were here.

I close my book. "I think I've got it. I'll keep working on it this weekend, but at least I know the proper way to say everything now." I ignore her and glance at my phone, which is loaded with texts. From girls. And Logan and Nick. And more girls. "I better get going."

"Um, okay. Yeah, me too," she says, glancing at her phone like there's something important in it. But I know better. If Dawson had texted her, she would have replied right away. And I haven't heard her phone ding or buzz since we arrived.

WE WALK TO the Cave in the moonlight. When we get to the clearing, I say, "Thanks for helping me. Have a good night."

Then I walk away, heading straight toward Nick and Logan, who are fortunately standing with a group of cheerleaders.

Unfortunately for me, a drunk Chelsea wraps her arms around my neck in greeting.

While her arms are still around me, I glance at Keatyn. She's standing alone. A quick look around tells me her friends are already paired off for the night.

"Let's get out of here, go back to your dorm," Chelsea says, slurring. She's even drunker than I thought.

"Um, hold that thought," I tell her, pushing her aside and grabbing a joint out of Logan's hand and taking a hit. Ashley bounces up to me, shoves her boobs out, and hands me a shot.

We clink our glasses and slam the shots together. Then she starts dancing in front of me, grabbing my hands and trying to get me to dance with her.

What the hell, I think, and break out a little arm shimmy, causing Logan and Ashley to cheer.

I MANAGE TO avoid both Chelsea and Ashley's blatant offers to hook up by telling them I have some catching up to do. I sit down in a circle on a log next to Logan. He starts telling a story about how we snuck out during our soccer camp last summer. I can't help but laugh and help him tell the story.

Keatyn is directly in my line of site though, and I watch as she talks to Shark and then my sister, the three of them sharing a joint.

I say I have to take a leak, leaving the group to go sit next to my sister. Shark hands me a joint. I don't think twice.

A girl leans down in front of Shark and whispers drunkenly, *Let's hook up.* He stands up, tells us, *Duty calls,* and leaves with the girl.

Peyton gives me a look. I nod at her, and she says, "There's Brad. I need to talk to him."

Leaving me sitting alone with Keatyn.

"Where's the harem?" she asks sarcastically, as her phone vibrates.

As she reads it, sadness washes over her face. Her phone drops to the ground.

I pick it up and read the messages.

Dawson: *I lobe you*
Keatyn: *I love you too.*
Dawson: *I druk.*
Keatyn: *You're drunk? Where are you?*
Dawson: *no shoes./'*
Keatyn: *Where are you?*
Dawson: *gurl bed partzy*

I can't help but shake my head as I hand her back her phone. She deserves so much better than this.

"Um . . ." She looks at me, like she expects me to say something reassuring, but I can't. I just feel bad for her.

And I wish that she knew I would never treat her like that.

I watch as she texts.

Keatyn: *Your brother is "druk," can't find his shoes, and is in a "gurl's bed at a partzy."*
Riley: *Shit.*
Keatyn: *Yeah.*

"Are you okay?" I ask her.

"Not really. Have fun with the harem. I'm heading back to my room."

"I'll walk you. The harem will wait."

She shakes her head. "No, I'm fine," she lies as tears form in her eyes. She turns around and runs through the trees.

I run after her. When she gets to her dorm window, she closes her eyes, leans against the side of the building, and starts to slide down into the grass.

I'm there to catch her. I pin her against the brick wall, slide my leg between hers, and push my chest tightly against her, holding her up.

She looks up at me, taking in my lips like she wants to kiss me.

I just shake my head, wrap my arms around her, and hug her.

Just hug her.

Which causes her to start sobbing. "I'm never, ever telling a guy I love him again. It's like I'm love cursed."

I nuzzle my face into her hair and whisper soothingly, "You're not love cursed. You just aren't—" I stop myself from saying it. I don't want her jumping from him to me just because she's upset.

"Just aren't what?"

I sigh deeply, barely believing I'm doing this again. "Maybe he's just drunk at the party. If he was hooking up, I doubt he'd stop to text you."

"I think the hooking up is over, and now he can't find his shoes."

"So you don't trust him?"

"What do you mean?"

"I mean, when he left, did you trust him?"

"I did. He told me over and over not to worry. To trust him. That he loves me."

"If he really loves you, he won't cheat on you. Even if he's drunk. You should have faith in the people you love. Maybe if you did, they wouldn't let you down."

She pulls out of my embrace and turns her back to me. "I'm going to cry alone in my room now. Thanks for your kind words," she says, but then she swings back around. And now, she's pissed. "So it's my fault if he cheats?! That sounds like the kind of zen bullshit the Keats guy would tell me. I didn't expect it from you. But I should have. It fits your whole player thing. The whole it's-never-my-fault, take-no-responsibility-for-your-actions-because-it's-easier-to-blame-fate, or cosmic forces, or someone else, than it is to admit that you just suck. Good night."

She needs to chill out. I run my hands down the sides of her arms, trying to calm her down a little.

"Boots, I didn't mean it that way. I meant that—" I shove my hands through my hair, trying to figure out the best way to say it. "Maybe the guy you're with isn't worthy of your love."

"Yeah, maybe."

Her phone starts buzzing and buzzing.

"Who is it?" I ask.

"It's Riley," she says, answering. "Hey, Riley."

She's still close to me, so I can hear their entire conversation.

"Where are you?" Riley asks.

"About to go in my room."

"Cam wants to talk to you. I've got him on conference with me. Say hi, Cam."

Cam says, "Don't be mad at him."

"He's texting me from a girl's bed!" she shouts into the phone. And I can't help but love it. Because she's right. It's bullshit.

"Yeah, a bed that he's in alone," Camden counters.

"No offense, Cam, but Riley told me about you. How you didn't think Dawson should have a girlfriend. I get it. You're a player. You want to have fun and not be tied down."

He laughs. "Actually, I'd love to be tied down." I hear him yell out to whoever is at the party. "Anyone got any rope? I want to be tied up."

"I said tied *down*," Keatyn says.

"Close enough," he replies with another laugh.

"It's been great talking to you," Keatyn says, still pissed. "Tell your brother when he sobers up not to bother calling me."

Go, Keatyn!

"And you need to cool your panties. He didn't hook up with anyone. In fact, he sucks as a wingman now."

"What do you mean?" she asks.

"He won't shut up about you. It's hard to pick up girls when one of us is all panty-whipped and talking about his amazingly hot girlfriend. So I did what I had to do. Got him drunk. Put him to bed." Shit.

Keatyn lets out an audible sigh and tears of relief flood her eyes. "He's really alone?"

"Yes. He's crazy about you. I'm not gonna let him screw that up. At least not until I meet you. I gotta go. Just got a taker on the rope."

Riley lets out a loud laugh. "You okay?"

"Do you think Cam's telling the truth and not just covering for him?" she asks.

"Yes, I do."

"Then, yes, I'm okay. Thanks, Riley."

She hangs up, and I look at her expectantly. Like I didn't hear what just transpired. I want her take on it.

"His brother said he's a bad wingman," she says. "That he kept talking about me in front of the girls. So he got him drunk and put him to bed."

I can't believe she'd forgive him that easily.

I cross my arms in front of my chest and clench my teeth to keep from going off. "Well, that's great."

"I'm going to bed now," she says as she climbs in through her window. Once inside, she sticks her head back out. "Thanks for following me. Checking on me. Trying to make me feel better. I appreciate it, Aiden."

"Can I ask you a question?"

She gives me a sassy grin. "You just did. But yes. Ask away." At least she's smiling again.

"What you said today in French. Do you think true love is bullshit, or do you believe in it?"

She looks up and sighs. "I really *want* to believe in it."

I want her to believe in it, too. I want her to allow herself to feel what's in her heart—her soul. But I realize in this moment, here, staring at the moon with my perfect girl, that I'm still not worthy of her.

A Keats' quote immediately pops into my head. 'I am profoundly enchanted by the flowing complexity in you.'

Which so describes her.

Everything about Keatyn is so complex.

I never thought earning her trust would be so complicated.

I never thought she would test my patience at every turn.

I need to stop trying to force it—just relax and be myself.

Let it evolve—and in the process, learn everything I can about her.

When we're together in moments like these—everything seems so simple.

But it's not.

There's another Keats' quote that goes like this: 'Two souls but with a single thought, two hearts that beat as one.'

I can't think of a more perfect way to describe how she makes me feel, because my heart has been beating for her since the moment we met.

I just need to be patient.

And, as much as I want to, I can't allow myself to sleep with her.

Not until she tells me the truth.

When we're finally together in that way, I want everything to be perfect.

She's looking up at the almost full moon shining above us.

"The moon is really pretty tonight, isn't it?"

She doesn't reply, seemingly lost in thought. The enchanted look on her face tells me that regardless of what she says, she does believe in fairy tales.

In fairytales, the prince always has to do something to earn the maiden's love, which means that I can't worry about her relationship status with anyone else. I'm going to have to woo her if I want to be her knight in shining armor—her prince, her true love, her fairytale.

Because what I want more than anything is for us to be able to look back someday and say: *And they lived happily ever after.*

But I can't tell her any of that just yet, so I just smile at her. "Don't let my sister go crazy shopping tomorrow."

She laughs. "I won't."

"Night, Boots."

Books by Jillian Dodd

The *USA TODAY* bestselling series,
The Keatyn Chronicles®

Stalk Me

Kiss Me

Date Me

Love Me

Adore Me

Hate Me

Get Me

Keatyn Unscripted

Hollywood Love Series

(A Keatyn Chronicles Spin off)

Fame

Power

Money

Sex

Love

That Boy Series

That Boy

That Wedding

That Baby

The Love Series

Vegas Love

Broken Love

Spy Girl Series

The Prince

The Eagle

The Society

About the Author

Jillian is a *USA TODAY* bestselling author who writes fun romances with characters her readers fall in love with, from the boy next door in the *That Boy* trilogy to the daughter of a famous actress in *The Keatyn Chronicles* to a kick-ass young assassin in the *Spy Girl* series.

Jillian lives in a small Florida beach town, is married to her college sweetheart, has two grown children, and two Labrador Retrievers named Cali and Camber. When she's not working, she likes to travel, paint, shop for shoes, watch football, and go to the beach.

FOLLOW JILLIAN ON HER WEBSITE
www.jilliandodd.net

Made in the USA
Middletown, DE
29 October 2018